SLAVE TO THE ALIEN WOLF MONSTER PRINCE

PART 1-10

BEATRIX STEAM

Other Hot Stories by Beatrix Steam

Impregnated by the Alien Monster
Reincarnated for the Monster King
Tentacle Alien Husbands
Spicy Monster Boyfriend's Bundle
Banged by the Hive Aliens
Railed by the Demonic Monster
Tentacle Threesome
Tentacle Alien Monster Smutt
Tentacle Alien Sacrifice

Subscribe to Beatrix Steam new release notifications!

www.beatrixsteam.com/subscribe

Content Warning

This is an erotic monster romance novel for adults 18+. It contains numerous adult scenes along with mentions of slavery and abuse. Many of the romantic relationships between characters are not healthy.

CHAPTER 1

Soft…

That was Astrid's first thought when she ran her fingers through his highness' fur.

Prince Rama was twice the size of a human man with strong limbs and yellow eyes. Sharp claws extended from his fingers at will, and his entire body was covered in thick grey fur.

Unlike human slaves, he didn't need clothes to starve off the planet's frigid winds.

Astrid usually dressed in several layers to keep her pale skin warm. Her black hair extended past her shoulders, and she wore thick gloves while traveling around the palace halls.

It was only in the bathhouse with its humid steam, could Astrid strip down to her lowest layer, a short underdress that extended to her thighs. The outline of her bra and underwear were visible against the thin fabric.

For the past year, it had been her job to bathe the prince.

She lathered soap through his thick fur before washing it out with jars of water.

The prince usually sat back in the tub as she ran her thin fingers through his fur, but for the past week, something was different about him.

He was quieter and more withdrawn. He barely engaged in conversation or even looked at her. His muscles tensed up every time that she touched him.

Astrid swallowed her discomfort and tried to focus on her task. It wasn't a slave's place to ask personal questions.

Astrid silently washed his back and shoulders. She moved her hand to wash his lower stomach, but he quickly flinched away.

"That's enough, Astrid," the prince growled, deep voice echoing off the tiled walls.

"I'm sorry, your highness," Astrid spluttered, almost dropping the brush in her hand. "Have I done something to displease you?"

Prince Rama was silent for a moment before his shoulders relaxed. "No….no you haven't."

"Then I shall continue, your highness."

Astrid moved her hand back to his front, but he flinched away yet again.

"No, that's enough." Prince Rama didn't even turn to look at Astrid. "You're dismissed."

Astrid felt her stomach drop. She bowed and quickly gathered her things, silently leaving the bathhouse.

Astrid was bought by the palace soon after she turned twelve. Before then she was raised by elite slave traders who trained human children to serve galactic elites.

Humans were good with their hands and following orders. They were popular as slaves throughout the galaxy.

Humans aren't good for anything else, she was often told. *Without training, they're no better than animals.*

Astrid never dared to argue.

The Ramul were a powerful race. Their leaders lived in a giant palace erected from ice and stone.

Astrid moved quickly through the palace's large halls, lowering her head every time that the large wolf-like body of a Ramul passed by.

It was a slave's job to quietly complete all their tasks without getting in the way.

Astrid pulled her thick shawl closer to her body, hoping that no one would comment on her long black hair not being tied back properly.

"Astrid!" called a raspy voice.

Astrid turned to see the head slave Mari walking her way. The elderly human woman was dressed in an assortment of worn shawls. She'd been working for the Ramul longer than any other human in the palace.

"Come with me." Mari gently linked her arm with Astrid's to lead her away. "There are things that we need to discuss."

*　*　*

Mari's room lay in the center of the palace. It was located behind the kitchens with a narrow bed and small fireplace. There was a small table and chairs that Mari used when talking to the other slaves.

Astrid found it hard to shake the memories of being scolded when she first arrived.

"Whatever it is, I'm sorry," Astrid said quickly. "I'll try harder."

"Hush," Mari said with a gentle smile. "You haven't done anything wrong."

"Then what is it?" Astrid nervously clasped her hands in her lap.

Mari let out a sigh. "Prince Rama is maturing. He's reached the stage where he's begun to…….have urges to breed."

"Oh," said Astrid. It wasn't what she had expected to hear.

"The king and queen have asked me to procure him a bed slave," said Mari. "It's best if he has a human to channel these urges instead of accidentally impregnating another Ramul."

Astrid nodded. "I see."

"I consulted the prince," said Mari. "And his first choice was you."

Astrid went silent as she attempted to process those words. It seemed ridiculous that someone as strong and powerful as the prince would have any interest in her.

"Sorry?" said Astrid. "Can you say that again?"

"I said that the prince would like to have you as his bed slave."

"Oh."

Astrid was hit by the mental image of the prince's large body hovering over her own. His throbbing erection pushing between her thighs.

Just the thought sent a pulse of electricity through Astrid's lower body.

"You don't have to if you don't want to," said Mari. "It would be easy for us to find a more willing participant…… and you can be assigned to another area of the palace to avoid any embarrassment. The choice is completely up to you."

"So if I don't agree….I'll be assigned to a different job?"

"It would be for the best," said Mari. "It's better if the prince's bed slave handles such things. We don't want him to…….pressure you into anything."

Astrid nodded, trying to imagine what her life would be like in the prince's bed. How often would he need to breed? What would it feel like to have his manhood thrusting in and out of her body?

What would it be like to climax around him?

"It's alright to think about it this evening," said Mari. "You can tell me in the-"

"I'll do it," said Astrid.

"Are you sure dear," Mari said kindly. "The Ra-mul can be quite demanding…especially one who is just maturing into a regular cycle. There's no shame in saying no."

"It's okay." Astrid looked straight into the elderly woman's eyes. "I'll do it."

Astrid was no stranger to sex.

Fornication wasn't forbidden between human slaves. It was accepted that they would breed and multiply unless desexed.

Astrid had never been cut, but she knew that if she were to have a child, there was no guarantee that they would be placed with a master as generous as the Ramul. They could be sold to a pleasure house, or sent to work the death mines of a distant moon.

She avoided most of the male slaves' shameless attempts at flirtation.

Except Forest.

Forest was a tall man with thick black hair and olive skin. His body was well built from working all day in the gardens.

Astrid found him visually appealing. He was an easy way to explore the new urges that pulsed through her body after puberty.

Forrest was also lonely.

He was used by slave traders as a breeder until too many of his offspring were born with deformities. He was soon sterilized and sold to the Ramul.

He went from impregnating fertile women all day long to a lowly gardener, banished to a small room in the green house which barely had room for a single bed.

But he still loved to fuck.

Astrid quietly lay back on his narrow bed as the muscular man thrust in and out of her dripping entrance, rubbing her clit with his fingers until she shattered around him.

The guy had a shit personality, but he was good with his hands.

Afterwards, Astrid lay back on the bed and watched Forest smoke opium. It was given to slaves who had a difficult time accepting their place.

"So… I heard that you agreed to be the prince's cumdumpster," Forest said with a long drag of his pipe, blowing the smoke directly into Astrid's face.

Astrid coughed, waving the smoke away with her hand. "Can news travel any faster around here?"

"What if he gets stuck in you?" Forest grinned. "I heard that Ramul dicks expand when they cum."

"I'm sure that it will go back down after a while."

"What if it doesn't? What if they have to cut you off him?"

"That won't happen," Astrid coughed.

"Are you gonna tell princey about the time that you let me stick it in your arse? I'm sure that he'll need all the tips he can get."

Astrid suppressed the urge to snap back at him. Such talk about their masters could lead to a whipping.

Astrid sat up and gathered her clothes. "Good night, Forest," she snapped.

"Why so defensive? Don't tell me that you actually want to fuck that monster?"

"What I want doesn't matter," Astrid coldly replied. "I'm only doing what's requested of me."

"Yeah, whatever," Forest muttered and took a drag of his pipe. "Enjoy sucking Ramul dick for breakfast."

Astrid rolled her eyes and quietly left the room.

Forest was often angry and bitter, but he soon mellowed out after his first hit, laughing to himself as he smoked the evenings away.

Astrid never wanted to become like him.

The next afternoon, Astrid was prepared for the prince's bed.

Her fellow slaves were silent as they washed and shaved Astrid's body.

There was a mixture of emotions on each of their faces. Pity, relief and even jealousy. The bed slave of a royal was a powerful position.

If Astrid survived it.

There was no telling what the prince would be like in bed. There would be no consequences for him if he damaged her body. Plenty of human bed slaves became incapable of having children.

After being covered in expensive oils and sprayed with perfume, Astrid was sent to wait in the prince's bed.

She lay naked under the sheets that she washed and changed the previous day, mulling over her new role in the palace.

She was to be a vessel for all of the prince's sexual needs from that evening onward. Her job was to happily accept his seed whenever he needed to empty himself. Refuse and she would be quickly replaced. There were countless power hungry woman who'd jump at the chance to be a prince's bed slave.

Astrid would protect him from them all.

After an hour, the prince's heavy footsteps echoed down the stone hall.

Astrid's heart rapidly beat in her chest as the large door swung open and the prince emerged.

He pulled back the sheets, running his dark eyes over Astrid's smooth curves and humble breasts, pausing at the neatly shaved space between her legs.

There was something in his eyes that Astrid had never noticed before.

A hunger.

"I didn't expect you to agree," he said, low voice causing a stirring in Astrid's core. "But here you are."

Astrid resisted the urge to rub her thighs together. "It is my duty to serve you, your highness."

"But not like this," said the prince, leaning forward to inhale her sweet scent. "This is a duty only for the willing."

"I am willing, your highness."

"Is that so?" he chuckled. "Are you ready to take me deep inside you, again and again until you're full of my seed?"

Blood rushed to Astrid's cheeks. "Of course, your highness."

"Good." The prince's tongue emerged from behind his sharp teeth, licking a long stripe up her naked neck. "Because once I start…I won't stop."

He was above her in an instant, running his warm tongue over her neck and collar bone, causing Astrid to shudder.

She gasped and tilted her head back, reaching out to take hold of his thick upper arms.

"I've wanted to do this for weeks," he moaned while moving down to lick her nipples. "Just your hands on my fur was enough to make me swell."

"Is.. that…so..your highness," Astrid panted, clenching her eyes shut.

"I wanted to pin you to the floor then and there. It's all that I've been able to think of for days."

Astrid nodded, clenching his fur.

Part of her had always wanted this too. She dreamed of having his strong body pressed against hers, rubbing her in ways that were forbidden, but she had always dismissed such thoughts as foolish fantasies.

Astrid could have never imagined that the prince wanted to fuck her too.

His tongue moved down her body, licking her stomach before dipping in between her thighs.

Astrid spread her legs out of habit, showing him her pink glistening cunt.

The prince didn't waste a moment, licking her center with vigor that she'd never experienced from a man.

Astrid gasped, pressing her hand to her mouth to muffle her cries.

It was heavenly.

His warm thick tongue felt perfect against her pulsing clit, creating delicious pleasure with every slide.

He enthusiastically slipped his tongue deep into her entrance, lapping up her essence like he couldn't get enough.

Astrid hissed and fisted the sheets, rolling her needy hips against his sinful mouth. Wave after wave of sensation consumed her lower half, making it impossible to think.

All that mattered was the slow build up of pressure in her core, growing larger and large with every press against her sensitive bundle of nerves.

"Delicious," the prince hummed while licking up and down her slit, holding her thighs to stop her from fidgeting. "Better than I could have dreamed."

It was too much.

Astrid couldn't hold back the pressure that burst from her center, driving her spiraling towards an all consuming orgasm.

Her body seized as she came, gasping and shaking as she rode the waves of her climax.

Prince Rama watched every moment.

"Did I do something wrong?" he asked, confused by her orgasm.

"No," Astrid laughed. "Not at all."

She pulled herself up and crawled across the bed towards him, lathering his face in kisses, all shyness washed away by her orgasm. "You just made me feel wonderful."

The prince hummed and rubbed his face against hers.

Something warm pressed against her lower body.

Astrid glanced down to see his cock.

The large pink organ gleamed in the faint light, fully erect and twitching with need.

This was what Astrid had been waiting for.

She reached down and wrapped her small hand around the pulsing dick, slowly running her fingers up and down.

The prince let out a low moan, glancing down to watch Astrid's hand move back and forth.

His reaction gave Astrid the confidence to continue, pumping her hand up and down as the prince shuddered beneath her.

His cock was damper than a human man's, dripping with fluid that made it easier for Astrid to pleasure him.

The prince let out a hiss and jerked away, pushing Astrid back on the bed. He climbed over her body, resting his weight on his forearms as he positioned himself between her damp thighs.

His thick cock rubbed against her soaked slit, bumping against her sensitive clit until it caught on her entrance.

He pressed inside, pushing in deeper with several small thrusts.

Astrid wrapped her arms around his neck, burying her face in his fur.

It wasn't painful like she expected.

Her dripping pussy stretched to accommodate his monstrous erection, taking it all the way inside with little resistance, filling Astrid to the brink.

The rub of his naked cock caused tingles of pleasure through her insides, making Astrid fidget and squirm.

The prince wrapped his arms around her body, holding Astrid close as he slowly pulled out, then slid back inside, thrusting his hips as he relished her wet heat.

The skin above his cock was bare and damp. It rubbed against Astrid's needy clit with every thrust, sending jolts of pleasure through her core.

Astrid wrapped her legs around the back of his thighs, angling her hips to get more addictive friction against her most sensitive area.

"So.....soft.." The prince moaned. "So warm and tight..."

His cock pressed against her cervix with every deep thrust, working her up to another all consuming high.

Astrid stopped trying to be quiet, letting out soft cries every time that his thick cock slammed deep inside her. Delicious pressure grew in her center.

The prince's breathing was heavy as he rocked his hips back and forth, allowing his needy cock to take him where he needed.

"I want to fill you up," he groaned. "I want to cum deep inside you all night long."

"Please... your highness," Astrid gasped. "Please use me as you wish..."

"You're perfect like this......all wet and damp for my cock. Nothing has ever felt as good as you."

Astrid gripped his fur as she felt another glorious climax begin to build in her center. She relaxed and gave into the sensation until her groin went numb, consuming her whole body in a pleasurable high, until she crashed, fighting for breath as she hugged the prince's body.

Her wet passage pulsated and sucked his cock deeper, milking the monster prince for all he was worth.

Prince Rama gasped as her cunt hugged him tightly. He thrust faster as he chased his own orgasm.

He pressed deep into her body as the base of his cock started to swell, locking them together until he unleashed himself with a groan, pumping wave after wave of hot cum deep inside her.

There was more than enough to fill Astrid and more, causing her womb to cramp as it stretched to accommodate his seed.

"Thank you.. your highness," she gasped, relishing in the sensation of having him locked deep inside her.

The prince groaned back as he shuddered against her. He basked in the waves of his orgasm as cum continued to spurt from his dick, immersing his mind in a relaxing warmth.

Astrid knew enough about Ramul biology to know that they would be stuck together for a while. It was best to just lay back and enjoy it.

The prince pulled out when he was finally through, collapsing beside her on the bed.

Cum leaked from Astrid's body and onto the sheets.

Astrid snuggled closer, dozing off against the prince's soft fur, basking in his warmth as he hugged her closer.

She knew that it was only the beginning. The prince would be consumed with the need to breed once more when he awoke. A young Ramul could be insatiable until he became used to his breeding cycle.

Astrid looked forward to helping him through it.

Chapter 2

Astrid huffed as Rama's giant cock pounded deep inside her.

She had been in the middle of helping him bathe when he insisted on ripping off her clothes, licking her naked skin before slipping his thick dick deep inside her.

"Your highness," Astrid moaned, watching his monstrous body move above her.

He was all that she ever wanted, large and strong with the power to break her.

Prince Rama's black fur was soaked and plastered to his skin. Saliva dripped from rows of sharp teeth. His thick pink cock pulsed as he rutted into Astrid's soaked pussy like a wolf in heat.

Her dark hair was soaked from the puddles on the tiled floor. Her tanned skin was covered in beads of water that the prince licked from her chest.

Astrid moaned and spread her legs wider to get more friction against her clit, grinding it against a wet patch just above the prince's dick.

She gasped.

It was wonderful, gifting her with joyous sensations that she'd never experienced with a human man.

The prince was insatiable. He had just begun his breeding cycle, so the need to reproduce was overwhelming. He was swollen and hard several times a day, making it difficult for him to continue his duties without some kind of relief.

Her warm wet body was the perfect hole for his hungry cock.

Astrid screwed her eyes shut as the sensations growing between her legs became overwhelming. She could feel his dick swelling in preparation for orgasm.

It stretched out her passage and filled her to the brim, triggering her own climax.

Astrid cried out as she came, thrashing against the floor as she clung to the prince's wet fur.

Every orgasm with him was pure bliss. Waves of happiness reverberated outwards from her core. Her soaked passage trembled and hugged him tight as Astrid's mind whited out.

She was addicted to cumming on his shaft.

The prince's monstrous dick continued to pound against her cervix, quickly thrusting as he chased his own high.

"*So wet*," he hissed while shoving himself as deep as possible and rolling his hips. "Always so wet."

His dick swelled to the point of no return, locking them together as cum sprayed out from the tip.

He unleashed in waves, pumping warm seed straight into Astrid's fertile womb.

She held the prince close as he shuddered and shook, riding the waves of his climax as he continued to empty himself inside her.

Astrid nuzzled his fur, enjoying the closeness and intimacy. It always felt good to hold him during sex.

The prince let out a sigh when he was through. He collapsed onto the wet floor beside her and relaxed into Astrid's hold.

He was still locked firmly inside her. It took some time for his cock to return to its normal size.

"Do you feel better, your highness?" Astrid asked.

Prince Rama nodded. "Yes, I always feel better with you." He ran his warm tongue along her wet cheek.

"Will we be leaving the bathhouse today, your highness?" she asked.

"No, I want to have you again on the floor, and then in the bath, and perhaps once from behind."

"Won't the water become cold, your highness?"

"I'll send for them to refill it. They can do it while watching me cum deep inside you."

Astrid let out a small laugh. "I don't think that's very appropriate."

"I don't care about appropriate." The prince rocked his hips like he was already hard and ready. "All I care about is unleashing my seed deep inside you."

He licked her earlobe before scratching his sharp teeth against it.

"Your highness," Astrid gasped. She usually needed more time to recover, but she didn't want to deny him.

The prince rolled back on top of Astrid, lazily thrusting his hips. His cum leaked out of her entrance, helping to lubricate every slide.

Astrid shuddered and held him close.

She never wanted these days to end.

Astrid limped back to her room an hour later.

She enjoyed the sex, but the prince was gigantic. It often took a toll on her body. There were several bruises on her hips and her groin was sore. She needed to return to her room to spread cream on her lower regions.

The prince's cum continued to drip from her body, pooling in her underwear. She was amazed that his body was capable of producing so much fluid.

"Astrid!" called an elderly voice.

Astrid turned to see the head maid Mari walking towards her. The elderly woman had cropped her white hair short, and there were several tattered shawls draped over her thin shoulders.

"Good Heavens, he has roughed you up," she said.

"I'm fine," said Astrid. "He can just be a little…enthusiastic."

"Yes, they all are," Mari muttered. She took hold of Astrid's upper arm and dragged her down a narrow hallway. "The king's grandfather was a notorious breeder. It is said that he fathered ten bastards by the end of his first cycle."

"Wow. That is a lot."

"And there were plenty more after that. It led to a terrible war after his death."

Astrid nodded. She had heard the story several times before. It was why the royal family began using human bed slaves.

"In here." Mari pushed open a battered wooden door.

Inside was a simple room with a bed and a fireplace. A red haired woman was sitting on the bed, sewing patches into her tattered clothes. Her skin was pale like the moon and covered in dark freckles.

She stood the moment that Mari and Astrid entered.

"Astrid, this is Flora," Mari said. "I take it that you know of each other."

"A little," said Astrid to Flora. "Weren't you one of the king's bed slaves?"

"Yes." Flora nodded. "For many years until he decided to release me. Now I just work in the kitchens."

That was a polite way of putting it. The king discarded all his old bed slaves and purchased a younger batch from slave traders.

"I was thinking that Flora could help you," said Mari. "She has much experience in pleasing the royal family, so I was thinking of assigning her to take on some of your duties."

"What do you mean?" Astrid asked.

"By having her help share Prince Rama's bed."

"I'm sorry…" said Astrid. The words went through her ears but her mind had trouble processing them.

"I'll pleasure him too," said Flora. "The old bed slaves and I had a system. The king would pick which one he wanted, and then that girl would go to him for the evening."

"Or perhaps you can take turns," said Mari. "Flora will tend to him in the morning, then you go to him in the evening."

"That could still be quite exhausting," said Flora. "I think it would be best to hire another girl or two."

"Perhaps you're right," Mari hummed. "The other old bed slaves should be able to handle the job."

"No." Astrid clenched her fists. "I don't need help."

"Don't be silly," said Flora. "The prince will ruin your body."

"No, he won't," said Astrid. "I'm fine on my own."

"Flora's right," said Mari. "The prince's needs are too much for one woman. It's better if you have one or more bed slaves to help."

"But I've been fine on my own," said Astrid.

"But don't you want to rest," said Mari. "Flora is very skilled and very capable."

"I'm especially good with my mouth," said Flora. "The king always chose me when he wanted someone to use their tongue."

Astrid ran her gaze over the other woman.

Flora appeared at least ten years older. Her breasts were larger and she seemed much more refined. She had years of sex experience that Astrid couldn't compare to.

But the idea of the older woman sucking the prince's cock was enough to make Astrid feel sick.

"I'm fine." Astrid's voice wavered. "Everything is going well, so I don't need your help."

Astrid spun on her heels and walked out of the room, slamming the door behind her. She didn't want to hear anymore about Flora fucking the prince.

They were wrong.

She could take care of all his needs on her own.

※ ※ ※

Astrid returned to the prince's room. He was sitting at his desk, trying to study as his pulsing dick stood swollen between his powerful thighs.

It twitched the moment that Astrid entered.

"Your highness." Astrid bowed and began removing her clothes, slipping off her shawls and dress. Thoughts of Flora swirled around in her mind.

How long would it be before Mari sent other women to the prince's bed?

"Is there something wrong," the prince asked. "You seem…sad."

Astrid sighed. Her upper half was bare and only her underwear remained. She shivered in the cold room.

Astrid picked up her dress and wrapped it around her shoulders. "They want….other servants to serve you in bed."

"Who said that?" asked the prince.

"The head maid."

"And is that what you want?"

Astrid shook her head before she realized that it could be too blunt. "I..I.. respect all of his highness' decisions."

"But is it what you want?"

Astrid's gaze fell to the floor. "I…I don't want the other servants to pleasure you."

The prince stood to his feet. "And why is that?"

Just the sound of his low masculine voice was enough to make Astrid's groin pulse. "I…I want to be the only one who serves you, your highness."

He stopped before Astrid. He reached one clawed hand out and tilted her face upwards.

Astrid suppressed the urge to cry. She needed to remain composed in front of the prince.

"Don't worry," said the prince. "You'll be the only one who serves me in bed."

"Really?" Astrid tried to suppress her joy.

"I've wanted you for so long." He wrapped an arm around her back to pull Astrid close. His throbbing cock pressed against her stomach. "And now that I have you, I don't want anyone else."

Astrid buried her face in his fur. It smelt of the soap that she used to wash him earlier that day. "Thank you, your highness."

"You drive me mad," he groaned with a roll of his hips, rubbing his needy shaft against her bare stomach. "All I can think about is being inside you."

Astrid let out a quiet laugh. "Let me help you, your highness."

She got to her knees, eyeing his twitching erection. Just the sight of the smooth pink skin and dripping tip were enough to make her wet.

She would prove to them all that Flora wasn't the only one in the palace capable of giving good head.

Astrid leaned closer and wrapped her small hands around the base of his shaft, causing the prince to let out a small hiss.

She opened her mouth wide, taking in as much of his dick as possible. It only got halfway in before it hit the back of her throat.

"*Fuck*," the prince hissed as his cock brushed against her warm lips. He rested a hand on Astrid's head, using her to anchor himself.

Astrid swirled her tongue around his pulsating length, moaning as she felt a familiar tingle of electricity between her own legs.

She sucked in her cheeks and bobbed her head back and forth, using her hands at the base to stop his erection from going in too deep.

The wolf prince watched on, gently thrusting his hips against her lips until it became too much.

"Stop," he growled and pushed her away. "Sit on the bed."

Astrid wiped the drool from her mouth and did as he commanded, taking a seat on the bed, heart racing in her chest.

The prince stood between her spread legs. He took hold of her thighs and pulled her closer, lining his dripping cock up with her entrance. He slowly pushed in, watching it disappear inside Astrid's warm body.

"This," he huffed. "Is the most beautiful thing in the world."

The prince paused to savor the sensation, shuddering as he resisted the urge to thrust.

Astrid hissed, gently rolling her groin to encourage him to move. It was excruciating to be left hanging.

The prince let out a sigh and rocked his hips, watching his cock move in and out of her soaked entrance.

Astrid closed her eyes and arched her back, fully giving her body over to the wolf monster prince.

His hands ran over her hips and breasts, studying every inch of exposed skin. "Humans are such wonderful creatures," he hummed. "The way that you feel inside is spectacular."

Astrid couldn't help but agree.

He pulled out. "On your hands and knees."

Astrid did as he commanded, getting on all fours and moving to the center of the bed.

The prince hungrily watched, eyeing her smooth behind. He crawled onto the bed and climbed over her body, slipping his dripping cock back inside her. His warm chest pressed against her back.

He groaned in ecstasy when he bottomed out.

Astrid hissed and gripped the sheets.

It was the prince's favorite position. His instincts screamed at him to dominate and breed on all fours.

He thrust inside her like an animal, fully giving into his primal urges.

Astrid cried out every time that his cock hit her cervix, trying her best just to remain upright. Her neglected clit pulsed between her thighs, but she didn't have the courage to touch it.

Her job was to please Prince Rama, not herself.

He growled and huffed while quickly rutting into her cunt, using her warm wet hole to satisfy his own needs. His dick pulsed and swelled inside her, locking itself into place to stop Astrid from fleeing.

The pressure was too much. It forced Astrid to climax. She cried out as she shook around him.

The prince let out a growl as fresh cum sprayed from his dick, flowing straight into Astrid's warm willing body.

He rested his clawed hands on top of her fingers, holding her hands tightly as his swollen cock continued to unleash inside her.

His weight pressed Astrid into the mattress, but she basked in the intimacy. Every wave of cum felt like proof of his affection.

The prince groaned and rolled onto his side, hugging Astrid tightly to his chest as his cock continued to empty out inside her.

Astrid felt her womb cramp as it stretched to accommodate all his seed.

He licked her face and neck. "So perfect," he hummed while gently thrusting his hips. "My perfect little human."

Astrid giggled and relaxed against him, already dreaming of what they'd do next.

Nothing could ruin this moment. Astrid would do everything in her power to stop another slave from having him.

Chapter 3

Astrid awoke to find herself lying in the prince's bed, thin sheets covering her naked body. The space between her legs was damp, white fluid still leaking from their activities hours earlier.

She rolled over to face him.

Despite his fearsome appearance, he was a handsome creature, with a regal bearing and a powerful presence that commanded attention.

Astrid had felt drawn towards him from the moment they met.

The prince slowly opened his eyes, his vision adjusting to the dim light of the room. He lay there for a moment, taking in his surroundings and stretching his limbs.

"Good morning, your highness," Astrid greeted.

He let out a low growl and licked her cheek.

She smiled and wrapped her thin arms around him in return. She hugged him close, feeling his warmth and heartbeat next to hers.

He let out a contented sigh and closed his eyes, enjoying the moment of peace and intimacy before the day's duties would call for his attention.

But there was also something else in need of attention.

His engorged shaft pressed against Astrid's side, dripping and begging for attention.

Astrid reached down to touch it, wrapping her small hand around the damp skin. She pumped her fingers up and down, eagerly creating joyous sensations with every slide.

The prince let out a growl, looking down to watch Astrid slowly pleasure him.

Astrid felt her own groin flare to life. She wanted to feel him, to have his hard shaft rubbing against her clit until she shattered.

The prince groaned and rolled on top of her, pressing their lower bodies together, enjoying the warmth and desire building between them.

Astrid wrapped her legs around him, their bodies entwining as they moved in sync, lost in the sensations.

This moment was special and unique. She wanted to make it last as long as possible.

Astrid moaned as his swollen cock slid through her dripping slit, covering itself in their fluids. She spread her legs wider, inviting him deep inside her.

His cock caught on her entrance and pressed inside, slipping in further with several small thrusts.

Astrid let out a soft moan as he moved inside her, their bodies rocking in perfect unison. Her nails dug into his back as she clung to his fur, her hips rising to meet his.

She was completely lost in the moment. Her mind and body focused on the sensation of him being inside her.

The prince let out a low growl, his primal instincts taking over.

He moved his hips like an animal, his movements wild and frenzied. He growled and gasped, his body writhing as he thrust into her.

Astrid moaned, body responding to his every move, muscles contracting around him.

He pushed into her harder and faster, his movements becoming more animalistic as he reached his own release.

Astrid relished every moment.

A powerful wave of pleasure built inside her. It started deep within her core and spread throughout her body, making her skin tingle and her breath quicken.

The sensation grew stronger, becoming almost unbearable as it reached its peak.

Astrid tensed, every muscle contracting as she let out a loud moan of ecstasy. Her whole world was consumed by joy as she reached her high, pleasure crashing over her in waves.

The prince sped up his thrusts, cock expanding and locking deep inside her.

The prince let out a deep growl of pleasure as he reached his climax, his thrusts becoming frantic as he emptied himself inside of her.

Astrid felt warmth spreading through her body, making her feel alive and desired.

They lay together, their bodies still joined, feeling the aftershocks of pleasure. The prince's cum continued to pump deep inside Astrid, trying to spawn a child that would never be.

The prince closed his eyes and drifted off to sleep, his arm still around Astrid as she lay next to him, enjoying the warmth of his body and the sound of his breathing.

Once the swelling of his cock had subsided, Astrid carefully slipped out of bed, trying not to disturb him as she gathered her clothes and got dressed.

Astrid cast one last glance at the prince before she left the room, closing the door quietly behind her.

✳ ✳ ✳

Astrid walked through the long cold halls of the palace, her mind still lingering on the night before. Just thinking of him moving inside her was enough to make Astrid's heart race.

The prince's seed dripped down her legs and she was covered in his fluids. She needed to use the slave's bathroom before it got crowded.

Unlike the members of the royal family, the female slaves shared one small room where they would strip naked and bathe.

Astrid turned the corner, only to see Forest walking in her direction.

The young man's eyes were glazed over and his movements were slow and unsteady. His clothes were wrinkled and unkempt, as if he had just rolled out of bed.

Forest's relaxed demeanour suddenly changed when he caught sight of Astrid.

He gazed over her disheveled hair and bruised skin, lingering on her stained clothes. It was more than obvious that she'd just been fucked senseless.

His face twisted into disgust.

"How kind of the prince's new bed slave to grace us commoners with her presence," he said, voice dripping with sarcasm.

"Stop that," Astrid hissed. "You're making a fool of yourself."

"Am I?" Forest grinned. "I hope you get nothing but respect for taking his highness' cum so well."

Astrid crossed her arms. He reeked of opium. It was more than obvious that he'd been smoking from the moment he awoke.

"I know a good spot just around the corner," Forest said. "Why don't the two of us have fun like old times?"

Astrid shook her head. "You know that I can't do that."

"Why not? You think you're above fucking me now that his dick has touched you?"

"My job is to please the prince."

"Using all the tricks I taught you?"

Astrid didn't reply. It was true that Forest had been her teacher. She knew little of sex before she began visiting his bed.

"I thought so," Forest huffed, taking her silence as a *yes*. He moved in closer, invading her personal space. "Don't you want some new moves to impress Princey? You wouldn't want him to get bored and move onto some other horny groupie, would you?"

"Quit it," Astrid snapped and pushed him away. "I'm not sleeping with you."

Forest let out a laugh. "You honestly think you mean something to that monster, don't you? Wake up and smell the snow, Astrid. You're just a flesh hole for a future tyrant."

"I'm not listening to this," Astrid muttered and spun on her heels, going back the way she came.

Forest's laughter echoed behind her. "We're all just tools to them, Astrid. Fucking tools."

"Stupid, Forest," Astrid muttered, face burning red.

He was going to get himself killed one day. Couldn't he understand how lucky he was to be placed with a royal family?

Astrid decided to forgo the bath and go straight back to the prince's room. After fighting with Forest she needed some kind of relief.

The prince was still asleep when she entered.

His large frame was sprawled out across the bed. The sheets were pushed aside, revealing his powerful muscles. He was a creature of raw power and danger, even as he slept.

Just looking at him made Astrid's pussy clench.

She slowly slipped off her clothes, letting them fall to the floor one by one, revealing her naked form. Her bones were prominent and her skin was smooth with faint bruises.

Astrid climbed up onto the bed next to the sleeping wolf monster prince.

She positioned herself between his legs, pressing her lips to the space between his thighs, kissing and licking his bare groin.

She could see his body responding to her touch. His shaft grew hard and swollen.

She felt a hunger growing within her, a need to be filled by him.

Astrid wrapped her warm lips around his growing cock, licking and sucking the skin, consuming all remnants of their previous love making.

It was Forest who taught her how to give head. It was Forest who taught her how to move with a cock deep inside her.

All Astrid's success so far could be attributed to him.

It was infuriating.

Astrid reached down to rub her pulsing clit, trying to ease the need that was steadily growing between her own legs.

Sex was an easy distraction from all her problems.

The prince groaned. He reached down to cup the back of Astrid's head, thrusting his sleepy hips up into her mouth.

Astrid tried her best to take him, gagging as his thick cock hit the back of her throat.

She wanted to be unforgettable.

Astrid pulled away and climbed over his body, pressing her lips to his.

The prince reached out and touched her waist, feeling the smoothness of her skin and the warmth of her touch. He wrapped his arms around Astrid and pulled her closer, enjoying the sensation of her body against his.

"I like the way that you wake me," he hummed, rolling his dripping erection against her. "I hope that this will be a regular thing."

Astrid giggled. "Only if you wish, your highness."

"I wish it very much."

Astrid pulled away, running her tongue along her lower lip. "Then let me indulge you."

The prince nodded.

Astrid straddled him. She lowered herself onto his dripping cock, fully taking him inside with little resistance.

The prince hissed.

Astrid closed her eyes, letting herself get lost in sensation as she moved back and forth, creating delicious pressure with every slide. Her swollen clit ground against the damp spot above his dick.

The prince watched her bare breasts bounce above him, groaning in pleasure as Astrid worked his body. He pulled her closer, his hips meeting hers with each thrust.

Astrid moved in a circular motion, pressing down on him as he thrust into her. She could feel the pressure building inside her as she moved faster and faster, her breath coming in short gasps.

Astrid moaned and threw her head back, body trembling with pleasure as she took everything she desired.

She felt completely consumed by him, lost in the intensity of their union.

Astrid's peak was intense, her body trembling and contracting around the prince as she reached the height of pleasure. A wave of warmth spread through her as she cried out, climax crashing over her like a wave. She clung to his fur tightly, her fingers digging into his skin as she rode out the aftershocks of her orgasm.

This was what she lived for.

The prince gripped Astrid's hips as her warm body convulsed around his rock hard shaft, sucking it deeper. He sped up his thrusts, pounding up into her damp heat as he chased his own end.

Astrid cried out with every slam against her cervix, bouncing up and down on his body.

As the prince reached his climax, his body tensed and his hips thrust upward, pushing deep into Astrid. His cock swelled and unleashed, filling her with his seed.

Wave after wave of thick cum sprayed forth, causing the prince to shudder and moan with ecstasy.

Astrid happily took it all.

Her body relaxed and she let out a soft sigh, feeling content as his seed continued to flow inside her.

She leaned forward and kissed his jaw, hugging the prince tightly as he continued to shudder and moan.

Eventually, the prince's fingers slowly slipped from her thighs as his body relaxed beneath her.

They lay together, enjoying the afterglow of their union.

Astrid felt satisfaction and pleasure as she lay on top of the prince, her body still humming from the intensity of their fucking.

As she drifted off to sleep, she felt a warmth in her heart, knowing that she was one step closer to making the prince her own forever.

CHAPTER 4

The palace garden was a peaceful retreat, a place for the royal family and guests to escape from the freezing world outside, and bask in the beauty of nature.

The greenhouse was filled with towering plants, exotic flowers, and bright fruit trees from different worlds. The air was humid, and the scent of blooming foliage filled the room.

Astrid lay sprawled out on the soft grass. Her pale skin glowed in the fake sunlight, and her dark hair fanned out around her head.

She was naked, plush breasts rising and falling with each gentle breath, smooth thighs glistening with fluid.

The wolf monster prince knelt between Astrid's legs, his imposing presence towering over her. The scent of freshly-cut plants mingled with his musky scent, filling her senses.

Astrid's fingers clenched around blades of grass as the prince's warm tongue traced a path over her skin, lathering her collar and breasts.

Her eyes fluttered closed as a shiver of pleasure rippled through her body. She let out a soft moan.

The prince's warm tongue moved between Astrid's legs, tracing her drenched slit. He groaned and lapped at her juices, eating her out as Astrid gasped and arched her back.

It felt like she was soaring through the clouds as intoxicating pleasure grew in her core.

The prince's large dick was swollen between his powerful thighs, flushed pink and dripping with fluid. It twitched with anticipation as the prince's tongue continued to trace Astrid's slit and clit.

"Please," Astrid moaned as she held back her climax. "I want to feel you inside me."

The prince nodded, climbing over Astrid's body. His throbbing cock pressed into her dripping hole, bottoming out with little resistance. He let out a sigh and began to thrust, enjoying the wet warmth of her pussy.

Astrid let out small gasps as the prince moved above her. The sensations he was eliciting from her body were intense.

He hit deep inside with each thrust, his powerful movements filled with raw animalistic energy that drove them both towards climax.

Astrid was powerless to resist the pleasure that was building inside her. She was pulled towards the edge of ecstasy.

The prince let out a deep guttural growl.

He was consumed by the needs of his cock, body moving in perfect unison with Astrid's as they both gave into their desires.

A familiar pressure grew in Astrid's core as the prince ground against her. It was beautiful and all consuming.

She held onto the prince's fur tightly and surrendered herself.

It exploded in a wave of euphoria. Her entire body was consumed by sensation, like she was lifted up and carried away on a tide of ecstasy.

She squeezed the prince tightly, unable to control her body's reaction. Her muscles contracted around the prince, pulling him deeper inside and intensifying the sensations for both of them.

The prince let out a growl of pleasure and increased his pace.

With a final, explosive burst of energy, he unleashed all his pent-up desire and pleasure. He let out a deep roar as he lost himself, body shaking and convulsing as he was consumed by the sensations coursing through his cock.

Astrid could feel his body pulsing and straining against hers. She wrapped her arms around him tightly, holding on as his cock expanded inside her.

Wave after wave of warm cum sprayed deep inside Astrid.

"It's good to see that you've become accustomed to breeding," said a deep voice behind them.

It shattered the moment. Astrid and the prince quickly turned to see who had spoken.

The prince's governess stood before them, an elderly wolf with grey fur and glasses. Her eyes narrowed as she took in the sight of Astrid's naked body and the prince stuck deep inside her.

"Your fiancé has arrived," the old wolf said in a voice devoid of emotion.

The prince's expression darkened. He growled low in his throat.

Astrid could feel the tension radiating off of him.

"She wasn't supposed to arrive so soon," the prince said, voice low and menacing.

The governess merely raised an eyebrow. "Your duties as prince do not allow for delays, regardless of personal feelings," she reminded him coolly.

The prince's jaw tightened, but he said nothing in response. Instead, he turned to Astrid, eyes filled with a mixture of anger and sadness.

"Come on," he said. "We should greet our guest."

The hangar was filled with sleek and shiny spaceships of all shapes and sizes. The sound of their engines echoed through the cavernous stone room.

The prince led the way, his steps confident and purposeful, until they reached a large silver ship that stood apart from the others.

Its sleek and graceful curves made it look like a work of art. Its numerous windows reflected the ships around them.

A long metal ramp extended from the ship's belly, touching the ground with a hiss.

The prince's fiancé was a formidable sight, with her pure white fur and towering height. She was dressed in shimmering silver battle armor that glinted menacingly. Her chest plate was adorned with intricate patterns and etchings that spoke of her conquests and victories in battle.

The human slaves accompanying her were dressed in luxurious attire, adding to the grandeur of the scene.

Astrid felt a shiver run down her spine as she realized the immense power and wealth that surrounded the prince and his soon-to-be mate.

The prince stood proud and tall, not showing a hint of nervousness or doubt as his future spouse strode down the ramp.

"We welcome you, Lady Rihna," bowed the prince's governess. "News has spread of your countless victories."

Lady Rihna huffed and looked down at the prince.

"Still a runt, I see," Lady Rihna said with a laugh. "I assumed you'd at least grow while I was off leading your family's seven year war."

The prince clenched his jaw, but remained silent.

"Lady Rihna," the governess scolded. "Such talk is not appropriate when addressing your future-"

Lady Rihna laughed. "What are they going to do? Throw me in a cell? Their next best general is a mindless buffoon."

The governess let out a growl and crossed her arms like she knew that the other wolf was right.

Lady Rihna raked her cool gaze over Astrid. "And what's this?"

"This is his highness' bed slave," the governess muttered.

Lady Rihna's expression twisted into disgust.

"I see," she said coldly. "Is this what you've reduced yourself to, my prince?" she added, turning to face him. "A human fucker?"

The prince straightened his back and raised his chin in defiance. "It is the monarchy's choice to have human bed slaves and none of your concern," he replied. "It has been decided to help keep the bloodline pure."

"Your choice?" Lady Rihna snorted. "This is not a choice, it's a disgrace. Why should I be expected to sleep with a being who could be harboring their filthy diseases?"

The prince's face darkened. "If you have a problem with my father's decisions, then you can take it up with him personally."

Lady Rihna narrowed her eyes. "You may be a prince, but you are still just a pup in my eyes," she sneered. "Enjoy fucking your 'bed slave,' but don't expect any entry into my cunt until you drop this bitch."

The prince gritted his teeth, but held his tongue.

With that, Lady Rihna turned and marched away. "I was promised a banquet if I came back to this frozen wasteland," she called to the servants. "I expect the queen to make good on that promise."

The dining room was grand and spacious, with high ceilings and ornate chandeliers that cast a warm glow over the stone walls. At one end of the room was a long crystal table where the queen was seated.

The prince's mother exuded a commanding presence. Her fur was glossy and well-maintained, and her piercing red eyes seemed to take in everything around her. She wore glittering gems, expensive necklaces, and rings that sparkled in the light. Her posture was impeccable, giving her an air of regality and power.

Lady Rihna approached the table, followed by the prince and the governess. They took their seats.

Servants brought out platters of food and poured glasses of wine.

Astrid stood with the other servants by the wall, quietly awaiting her next order. She kept her head down, avoiding any eye contact with the royal family, but her stomach growled as the scent of the lavish feast wafted toward her. She tried her best to ignore the delicious smells, reminding herself of her place in the hierarchy of the castle.

"Now that Prince Rama has come of age," said the queen. "We would like to have the joining as soon as possible."

Astrid clenched her hands. She found the idea of the prince marrying Lady Rihna mortifying, but she wasn't in a position to complain.

"I am the strongest warrior that you have," said Lady Rihna, her eyes flashing with anger. "Why must we be married so soon? I would be far more useful on the front lines, fighting for our people."

The queen sighed. "We understand your passion for battle, but the prince needs a strong mate to lead beside him. And you, with your victories and strength, are the perfect match."

Lady Rihna scowled. "I'm a warrior, not a breeder. I still have battles to win and territories to conquer."

"Lady Rihna, we understand that you may have qualms about the birth, but it is important that the prince produce an heir as soon as possible," said the queen.

"I'll be no use to anyone if I'm pregnant and weak," said Lady Rihna.

"The future of our kingdom rests on the prince's ability to breed. It is your duty as his future mate," the queen implored.

"I will not be burdened with the responsibility of carrying a child while I'm still in my prime," Lady Rihna declared, her voice firm.

The queen sighed and looked to the prince. "Rama, can you not convince your mate to fulfil her duties?"

The prince was quiet, seemingly uncomfortable with the conversation.

Astrid felt a twinge of sympathy for him.

"I will do my duty to the empire in the best way possible," Lady Rihna rose from the table. "And right now, that means remaining in the army."

She strode out of the dining room, leaving the others in stunned silence.

"That went better than I hoped," said the governess.

"Don't worry," said the queen calmly. "She'll change her mind once the king returns."

The prince and Astrid made their way back to his room in silence. The prince was tense and Astrid could sense that he was troubled by the conversation at the banquet. She could feel the weight of the upcoming marriage and the responsibilities that came with it pressing down on him.

As soon as the door closed behind them, the prince took Astrid by the shoulders, pushing her towards his desk. He bent her over the hard surface, rolling his throbbing erection against her soft arse.

Astrid gripped the desk and tried her best to remain standing.

The prince tugged at her dress, hiking it up above her waist and ripping down her underwear to expose Astrid's dripping cunt. He slid his pulsing cock deep into her wet heat, letting out a sigh as he quickly thrust.

Astrid struggled to keep up with his pace, her breaths coming out in gasps as he pushed her to the brink. Despite the discomfort, she couldn't help but feel a deep-seated pleasure as the prince claimed her body, taking out his frustration and pent up desire on her.

In the end, she cried out in both pain and ecstasy as she reached her climax. The prince followed shortly after, and they both collapsed onto the desk, gasping for air.

The prince hugged Astrid close as his cum continued to empty out inside her.

Astrid tried her best to comfort him, rubbing circles against the back of his hand.

"Are you alright, your highness?" she asked.

The prince didn't respond, lost in the pleasure of his climax. He pulled out once his cock shrank back down to its regular size.

Astrid gently touched his shoulder and asked again. "Your highness, are you alright?"

The prince sighed and took a seat on his bed. "Lady Rihna was supposed to marry one of my brothers. But now that they're dead, the burden has fallen on me."

"So I've heard," Astrid said softly. "The other servants often speak of their strength."

"But they died in battle," the prince said. "They were both excellent warriors, but it wasn't enough."

Astrid shuddered. She wished there was something she could do for him.

The prince looked up at Astrid. "Thank you for being by my side," he said, voice barely above a whisper.

Astrid smiled softly. "I'll always be here for you, your highness. I'll do whatever I can to help."

The prince reached out and took Astrid's hand.

For a moment, they sat there in silence.

Astrid felt her heart skip a beat as she looked at the prince, her feelings for him growing stronger with each passing moment.

But as quickly as the moment came, it passed, and the prince stood up, letting go of Astrid's hand.

"Thank you," he said. "But I would like to be alone now."

Astrid nodded, watching as the prince climbed into bed and settled under the covers.

As she turned to leave, Astrid felt a sense of longing in her heart, knowing that she could never truly be with the one she loved.

❄ ❄ ❄

Astrid knew that it was wrong to spy on Lady Rihna, but she knew no other way of helping the prince. She crept silently towards the guestroom door. The need to find out what the large wolf was doing was too strong to ignore.

As Astrid pressed her ear to the door, she heard muffled sounds coming from within. She swallowed hard and carefully pushed the door open, peering through the crack to see what was happening.

What she saw made her heart race.

Lady Rihna was embracing a human slave woman, pulling her close while licking her neck.

The human slave was beautiful with pale skin, long blond hair, and wide hips. Her lips were full and pink.

She was fully naked, thighs spread wide to invite the large wolf between them. Her delicate hands pressed against Lady Rihna's chest as the wolf monster nuzzled into her neck.

"Lady Rihna," the woman moaned.

Lady Rihna pressed her mouth against the slave's neck, grazing her teeth lightly over the skin.

The slave gasped and shuddered, her fingers digging into Lady Rihna's fur as she held on tightly.

Lady Rihna's hands roamed over the slave's body, pulling her close and pressing their groins together in a slow sensual dance. She rubbed her engorged clit over the human woman's drenched cunt, using the human's warm fluids to drive her own pleasure.

The human woman groaned and arched her back, gasping as Lady Rihna's clit rubbed against her own.

The room was filled with the sound of their breathing, heavy and ragged, as they moved together in a hypnotic rhythm.

Astrid felt a flush rise in her cheeks as she watched, feeling like an intruder on something that was meant to be private.

Lady Rihna moved faster, growling as she relished the woman's wet heat.

The human slave threw back her head and let out a loud moan. Her body trembled with pleasure as Lady Rihna's touch sent waves of sensation through her.

Lady Rihna's movements were powerful and controlled, driving the servant to new heights of ecstasy.

The slave's eyes rolled back in her head as she surrendered herself to the sensations coursing through her body. Lady Rihna's powerful grip on her hips only intensified as she pushed them both to the brink.

Lady Rihna cried out as she climaxed, rapidly thrusting into the other woman's groin as she gasped for breath.

The human woman's body trembled with her own climax as they both rode waves of pleasure, their bodies intertwined as they sought their release.

As the peak of their passion subsided, Lady Rihna's muscles relaxed. She pulled away from the slave, who was limp and panting. Lady Rihna's gaze was intense, a mixture of satisfaction and pride, as she looked down at her conquest.

Astrid, realizing that she had stayed too long, silently retreated from the door.

Astrid found the prince lying in bed, staring up at the ceiling with a distant look in his eyes. He seemed lost in thought, and Astrid couldn't help but feel a twinge of sadness for him. She took a step closer to the bed and cleared her throat.

"Your highness," she said softly. "I'm sorry to interrupt, but I have news."

The prince turned his head to look at her. "What is it?"

"I saw Lady Rihna in her room," Astrid said, trying to keep her voice steady. "She was with a slave, a human woman. They were......pleasuring each other."

The prince's face darkened, and he looked away from her. "I see," he said. "So even Lady Rihna could not resist bed slaves."

Astrid nodded. "I think that I know a way of helping you."

"Really?" said the prince. "How?"

"I could carry your offspring," said Astrid. "I can be a surrogate for your children with Lady Rihna."

"That's a noble offer," the prince said. "But it's not necessary. I will do my duty as the future king, even if it means joining with her."

"But your highness, you deserve happiness," Astrid protested.

"I appreciate your concern, but this is my burden to bear. My kingdom and my family come first. I will make the best of the situation and find a way to make it work."

Astrid sighed, searching her mind for a way to convince him.

"But it's something I think of a lot," said Astrid. "I dream of being pregnant by you."

The prince went silent for a moment.

"It's something I think of too," he said. "I fantasize about you being round and swollen with our young."

"You won't have to fantasize anymore," said Astrid, kissing his hand. "Because I can help make it a reality."

"Are you sure?" asked the prince, his eyes searching hers. "It won't be easy. It could even kill you."

"I'm positive," said Astrid, voice strong and determined. "I want to help you and the monarchy."

The prince pulled Astrid into a tight embrace. "Thank you," he whispered. "You've given me back my hope."

He rested his head against Astrid's stomach.

She ran her fingers through his fur, feeling the soft strands against her skin. He wrapped his arms around her waist, hugging her tightly as they stood there in comfortable silence.

The prince nuzzled her stomach. "Humans truly are amazing creatures," he hummed. "Your body is extraordinary."

The prince pulled up Astrid's dress, running his warm tongue over her smooth stomach.

Astrid moaned, overwhelmed by the sensation.

His fingers traced the curves of her hips and thighs, sending shivers down her spine.

The prince pulled Astrid back onto the bed and climbed over her body, running his tongue along her exposed neck.

She arched her back, pressing herself closer to him, and he growled softly in response. His hot breath on her skin sent waves of desire through her. She tugged at his fur, pulling him closer.

Astrid spread her thighs to allow the prince to rest between them, grinding her hungry core against his hard body.

The prince let out a growl in response, rolling his pulsing erection against her.

Astrid fumbled with her clothes, pulling down her underwear to allow his thick dick inside her.

The prince's cock slotted in like they were made for each other, bottoming out with several small thrusts.

"I can't wait to see you round and full with my pups," the prince groaned with a roll of his hips. "I want to feel them move inside you."

Astrid nodded. It was nice to imagine that he was impregnating her at that moment, that his seed was capable of planting a child inside her human body.

She held him close as his dick rocked in and out, enjoying the intimacy of his body against hers.

The prince huffed against her hair, speeding up as his climax approached. His cock expanded inside her, forcing Astrid to orgasm.

She gripped him tightly as pleasure exploded outwards from her core, causing her body to seize and shudder.

The prince's cum flowed into her body, trying to create a child that could never be.

Astrid found it nice to imagine that she could already be pregnant.

"Thank you," she smiled.

The prince hummed and nuzzled her hair, basking in the post orgasm high.

Astrid closed her eyes and let out a contented sigh, hoping that her love and sacrifice for the prince would pay off one day.

Chapter 5

The prince and Astrid lounged on a plush velvet lounge in the corner of his bedroom. The flickering light from the fire cast a warm glow over the wall, creating a cozy atmosphere.

Astrid rested her head on the prince's chest, listening to the steady rhythm of his heart. He ran his fingers gently through her hair, enjoying the feeling of the soft tresses against his fingertips.

Astrid was content to just lie there, listening to the rise and fall of the prince's chest. She closed her eyes and focused on the sound of his breathing, letting the peacefulness of the moment wash over her.

The prince spoke up, breaking the silence. "You look so beautiful in this light," he said, gazing down at her with admiration in his eyes.

Astrid smiled up at him. "And you look handsome as always." She stroked his furry cheek with her fingertips.

She wasn't sure when she'd first felt attraction towards him, but her dreams had been filled with his presence and body soon after she was assigned as his slave.

She saw his large throbbing manhood as he bathed, thick and erect with need. She couldn't help but imagine it filling her passage, thrusting in and out as his large muscular body held her down.

She knew that she should fear him, but she could not help but be drawn to him like a moth to a flame.

It was an honor to have been chosen as his bed slave.

The prince's arms encircled Astrid's waist as she climbed onto his lap.

She leaned her head back and looked up at him. The warmth of his body radiated through her. She nuzzled her cheek against his broad chest.

"You feel bigger," he said, running his large hands over her back and hips.

Astrid smiled and snuggled closer. "It's because I have your babies inside me." She placed a hand on her pregnant belly.

The prince's palm immediately went to her stomach, rubbing it gently. "I can't wait to meet them," he said softly.

Lady Rihna had been more than happy to hand over her eggs before leaving for war. She didn't care what they did with them, as long as she could continue her campaign.

Astrid's body had been pumped full of fertility drugs to handle the implantation. Her once thin frame had become voluptuous and curvy, with her hips and thighs swelling to a fuller shape. Her clothes no longer fit her properly, stretching around her middle.

One of the most striking changes in Astrid's body was the swelling of her breasts. They had doubled in size, filling out her chest band to the point of bursting. The weight caused an ache in her chest, but Astrid felt proud of their new size.

The prince also seemed to enjoy them.

His fingers lightly trailed over Astrid's stomach. The warmth of his touch made her squirm. She looked up at him, meeting his gaze with a soft smile, pretending that it was their babies inside her, not the spawn of his ferocious fiance.

He cupped her engorged breasts, feeling their weight and warmth.

Astrid arched her back, pressing her chest into his hands, inviting him to touch her as he wished.

The prince leaned in and licked her lip, his tongue seeking entrance into her mouth. His hands roamed over her body, exploring every curve and swell.

Astrid jolted as the prince's sharp teeth brushed her lip. She let out a soft gasp, the sound muffled by the press of their mouths. Her hands slid up to tangle in his fur.

The prince let out a deep groan as Astrid rolled her hips against him. His cock grew harder with each passing moment. His hands moved to grip her hips, holding her steady as his tongue plundered her mouth.

Astrid rocked against him, using his powerful body to ease the hunger inside her. Her breathing was shallow and soft, the pads of her fingers spread over his heart.

The prince's throbbing arousal swelled between them.

Astrid's lips curved into a smile as she ground her hips against his erection. She could feel the power and strength of his body. It only made her want him more. She arched her back, pressing her breasts against his chest, silently begging him to take her.

The prince broke the kiss to look into Astrid's eyes, his own dark with lust. "I need to be inside you," he breathed, voice husky. "Now."

Astrid nodded, pulling up her dress. Her lower half was bare, still dripping with his essence from their love making hours earlier.

The prince grabbed Astrid's breast band, lifting it up and over her head. He took in her naked body, eyes lingering on her swollen breasts and the curve of her pregnant belly.

His rough tongue moved down Astrid's neck and chest, licking every inch of skin. His hands moved to her hips, gripping them tightly as he spread her legs apart.

Astrid was dripping with anticipation. Every second that she had to wait was excruciating. She wanted to be used for his enjoyment and screwed senseless.

The prince positioned himself at her entrance, slowly pushing his swollen member inside her delicate folds. Astrid let out a gasp as his cock filled her completely, stretching her tight hole around him as he pushed deeper.

The prince's hips pressed against Astrid's, their bodies intertwined, skin against skin. His cock pressed fully inside, relishing the tight wetness that enveloped it.

The prince's breathing was heavy. A low growl came from deep within his throat. "You're so soft," he moaned with a roll of his hips. "All swollen and perfect for my young."

Astrid hissed, rocking her hips against him, meeting the prince thrust for thrust, feeling his body swell and throb deep inside her. Her engorged breasts shook with each push of his hips.

The room was filled with the sounds of their bodies slapping together as they lost themselves in each other.

The prince clenched his eyes shut, focusing on the growing sensations in his dick. He wrapped his arms around her tightly, pulling her closer as he lost himself in the moment.

Astrid let out a soft moan, relishing in the pleasure that coursed through her. Her hands roamed over his chest, feeling the muscles tense and relax with each movement.

She arched her back, body pushing against his as she ground her needy clit against his groin. Pressure grew in her core, building with each delicious slide.

Intoxicating tension coiled within her, the anticipation of release causing her to grip him tighter. Astrid gasped sharply as she felt the pressure in her core build. Her warm passaged tightened around him.

"The way you feel around me," he moaned, "I can barely hold back."

The prince's speed increased, driving deeper into Astrid's body with each thrust.

Astrid could feel anticipation coursing through her veins, the promise of pleasure dancing just out of reach.

The prince buried his face in her neck, kissing and nipping at her skin as his climax approached.

Astrid couldn't help but feel satisfied for bringing him such pleasure.

The prince swelled inside her, spiraling towards release. He quickened his pace as he thrust in and out, chasing the rapidly growing high.

Astrid gripped the prince's forearms, using them to brace herself against his driving hips. She felt him swelling and throbbing inside her, pushing her to climax.

Astrid let out a gasp as his hot seed erupted inside her. Her body jolted at the sensation, hips grinding against his. Her legs quivered as she let out a long sigh of bliss, riding out the waves of her climax.

There was no better feeling in the world.

She leaned forward and placed a soft kiss on his lips, feeling the warmth of his body as his cum sprayed inside her.

The prince hissed and clenched his eyes shut as he was hit by another wave of sensation.

Astrid felt jealous that his people were capable of experiencing such long drawn out pleasure.

Eventually, the prince's breathing slowed and he opened his eyes. "You're so beautiful," he said softly, hand rubbing soothing circles on her back.

Astrid smiled, feeling warmth spread through her body at his words. She leaned down to kiss him again, feeling a renewed sense of desire coursing through her. The prince responded eagerly, pulling her close and deepening the kiss.

As they broke apart, the prince ran his hands over Astrid's body, exploring every inch of her with a tenderness that took her breath away.

There was no doubt that she was truly in love with him.

Astrid still ate dinner with the other slaves.

The dining room was located beneath the palace. The dim flicker of candles cast ominous shadows on the worn wooden tables.

The room was crowded with human slaves dressed in tattered clothes, their hushed conversations creating an eerie buzz.

Their meals were a thick grey powder that had been created using ingredients from the human homeworld.

The slave traders told Astrid that the humans who remained on Earth were speechless animals who walked around naked and lived in trees. They barely made it to adulthood before being devoured by the fearsome beasts who roamed the planet.

The slave traders assured Astrid that she was lucky to have been plucked from obscurity and taught how to talk. She'd have a chance to experience a long life in return for serving her masters.

Astrid found herself a seat at a table near the back of the room. She tried not to let her discomfort show as the other slaves stared and whispered to each other.

"Is that her?"

"I'm surprised that she's still alive?"

"How much longer do you think she'll last?"

"That monster's spawn will probably rip her body apart."

Astrid felt a shiver run down her spine. She knew that the others resented her, jealous of her position as the prince's lover and the surrogate of his children.

Her heart sank when she caught sight of Forest. He laughed and joked with other slaves like she didn't exist.

Astrid tried to avoid his gaze, not wanting to give him the satisfaction of knowing how much he still affected her, but she couldn't help stealing glances at him every now and then.

He looked much better than the last time she saw him. His hair was cut shorter, and he had put on some muscle. But when he glanced towards Astrid, his gaze was cold and distant, making her realize that nothing had changed between them.

Astrid took a deep breath, trying to steady her nerves, then turned her attention back to her food.

She didn't have much of an appetite, but she knew she needed to keep up her strength for the babies.

A kind voice spoke up, cutting through the noise. "Ignore them. They're just jealous."

Astrid turned to the voice. "Thank you, I-"

The words died in her throat when she realized that it was Flora, the ex-bedslave who Mari tried to assign to the prince's bed.

Flora's long red hair was tied back in a bun. There was a thick shawl draped over her shoulders to ward off the palace chill.

They hadn't spoken since Astrid stormed out of Flora's room, declaring that *she was enough to attend to the prince's needs.*

Flora took a seat beside Astrid. "It was like this for me too when I was in the king's favor. They despise anyone who gets any special treatment from the royal family."

Astrid nodded. In the past she was also the same, whispering gossip about the royal's favorite bed slaves.

"Why are you doing it?" Flora asked.

"Doing what?"

"Carrying his babies. You know that it could kill you, right?"

Astrid bit her lower lip. She tried to put her feelings into words. It was hard to explain. It was more like an instinct. She wanted to be closer to the prince and be the center of his world. Birthing his children seemed like the best thing to do.

"It's my duty to make him happy," said Astrid.

Flora let out a sigh. "I've seen plenty of girls like you in the king's bed. They thought that if they over exerted themselves there would be some kind of reward in the end, but there was nothing. We're just toys to them."

"No, you're wrong," Astrid said.

Flora didn't understand the prince. She didn't understand the bond between them. He wasn't like his father.

"I'm only telling you this so that you won't be disappointed," said Flora. "Once he works out that he can have his pick of women, he'll just–"

Astrid shoved her meal away and got to her feet. "Stop," she hissed. "Just stop talking. You don't know anything about me or him, so don't pretend like you do."

"It's not like that," said Flora. "I just–"

Astrid stormed out of the dining room, her heart racing with anger and frustration. How dare Flora speak to her like that? How dare she insinuate that the prince was just using her?

Astrid would prove them all wrong. She'd show everyone that what she had with the prince was special and that the two of them belonged together.

*** *** ***

Astrid's pregnancy progressed quickly. Wolf pups developed faster than humans. Her stomach expanded over the coming months, but it didn't kill her desire for the prince's cock.

She spent most of her days naked in the royal's bed, laid back on the sheets as his thick dick thrust deep inside her. Despite her pregnancy, she still wanted to ease his sexual needs. Her large swollen stomach and engorged breasts made him hornier than ever.

"Yes, yes, yes," Astrid gasped as she lay on her side, allowing the prince to take her from behind. His large body was flush against her back, one hand resting on her swollen stomach as his pulsing cock rocked in and out of her soaked pussy.

The prince grunted, face contorted into something primal. His fingers dug into her hips as he continuously took her.

They didn't care about being careful anymore. Astrid was already past her due date. They hoped that the rough exercise would help bring on the labor.

Astrid's stomach was stretched to its limit, accommodating the two wolf babies that were growing inside her.

Her swollen breasts were three times their regular size, bouncing with the pounding of the prince's hips. Clear fluid dripped from the nipples, trickling onto the sheets below her.

The prince pulled out and rolled Astrid onto her back. His rough tongue licked her chest, lapping up the warm fluid dripping from her breasts. His eyes locked on hers as she gasped and moaned.

"Delicious," he groaned. "All full and ready."

The prince moved down, taking each nipple in his mouth, sucking on them tenderly as his sharp teeth scratched her skin.

The prince's cock thrust back inside Astrid, slapping her pussy as he rocked in and out.

Astrid groaned, her fingers clutched the prince's sheets. Her toes curled in ecstasy as she soared to the edge of release.

She could feel the heat radiating from her core. Her body was trembling with pleasure, and she knew that the prince wouldn't last much longer.

Astrid arched her back, pressing her swollen stomach against the prince's warm body. Her head tilted back as he drove in one last time, filling her with his warm seed.

Astrid cried out. A fuse of pure pleasure ignited inside her. It drowned out her consciousness, and the whole world melted away.

The prince held himself there as his swollen cock twitched and throbbed inside her, spraying his essence deep into her passage, watching as she shattered around him.

He reached a hand toward her stomach, feeling the babies move inside her.

"You'll be such a perfect mother," he whispered.

Astrid smiled. Her heart swelled with happiness. After so many years of struggling she finally had a place where she wasn't just invisible or a tool.

She had someone who loved her.

CHAPTER 6

Astrid pressed her fingertips against the laboratory window, her breath fogging up the glass.

Inside, two small wolf pups snuggled in the arms of their wet nurse. They were delicate and tiny with snow-white fur that sparkled under the bright laboratory lights. Every feature, from their sharp snouts to their piercing blue eyes, reminded Astrid of Lady Rihna. However, it was impossible to tell if they would grow to be as large and powerful as their mother.

Astrid felt a sense of wonder and amazement as she watched the tiny creatures. She couldn't help but smile as they wiggled and nuzzled the wet nurse.

Astrid's body ached from giving birth. She was still bleeding heavily, and her breasts were swollen and full of milk that the pups couldn't drink.

The labor had been intense, but she couldn't remember most of it because of the drugs that they pumped through her system. She vaguely recalled silhouettes of doctors around her bed as they pulled each of the children from her belly, with no words of sympathy or congratulations, only hushed admiration for their successful implantation. She knew it was a miracle that any of them had been born at all.

Despite the pain, Astrid couldn't tear her eyes away from the babies. She had carried them inside her for months, feeling them grow and kick, and now they were here, tiny and perfect.

Even if she wasn't allowed to care for them anymore.

"They are beautiful, aren't they?" the head slave Mari said softly. "Lady Rihna and the prince have given us two strong and healthy pups."

Astrid nodded, still mesmerized by the babies. "Yes, they are," she murmured.

Mari wrapped an arm around Astrid's shoulder, gently guiding her away from the glass enclosure.

"Come now," Mari said in a soothing voice, "it's time for you to rest."

Astrid nodded, tearing her gaze away from the window. She knew that Mari was right, but she couldn't help feeling a sense of longing as she walked away, leaving the babies behind.

Mari guided her down a dimly lit hallway, their footsteps echoing on the stone floor. They passed several other slaves, who stared and whispered to each other, until they arrived at Mari's room.

Mari helped Astrid sit down on the bed, pressing a hand to one of Astrid's engorged breasts.

"These seem full," said Mari. "Have you been squeezing the milk out every few hours like I instructed?"

"When I remember," Astrid mumbled.

"Make sure you do," said Mari. "If you allow the milk to build up, it could lead to an infection."

Astrid nodded. It was a lot to remember. Her mind was still hazy from the birth, but there were so many things that she needed to do to take care of herself.

"Has the prince come to see them?" Astrid asked.

"He came this morning." Mari moved about Astrid's room, picking up blood-stained clothes to wash. "He looked overjoyed."

"That's good," Astrid said, trying to hold back tears.

It was beneath the royals to visit a slave's room. She wouldn't be able to see him until she was better.

"The queen also seems pleased," said Mari. "And the king… well… it can be hard to tell what he thinks."

Astrid's eyes welled up with water. She buried her face in her hands.

Mari let out a sigh. "I know, dear, but the feeling will pass."

Astrid shook her head. "No, it won't. I carried them for months. I should be there beside them."

Mari sat down on the bed beside Astrid. "Every mother feels this way, but they're the royal family's children, not yours. You've done our duty, and now it's time to hand them over."

"Then how do I stop feeling this way?"

"With time." Mari rubbed Astrid's shoulder. "You'll learn to move on."

Astrid wiped away her tears and took a deep breath. "You're right. I'm sorry."

Mari smiled gently. "There's nothing to apologize for. Let's get you some rest."

Mari was Astrid's constant companion, bringing her food and medicine, but Astrid constantly thought of the prince. She missed his warm comforting presence.

"Maybe I can go talk to him for a moment," said Astrid. "Just to see how he's doing."

"My child," Mari said with a shake of her head. "What good are you to him like this?"

"But I feel a lot better now," said Astrid. "I can do it."

"There's no need to exert yourself," said Mari. "He's in good hands."

"What do you mean?"

"Don't worry yourself." Mari helped Astrid get into bed. "He only wants you to focus on getting better."

Astrid nodded and closed her eyes, imagining how happy the prince would be to see her once they were reunited again.

As days passed, Astrid's body slowly healed. The deep pain in her chest and abdomen started to subside, and the bleeding became less severe. She still felt weak, but she could now take short walks without feeling exhausted.

Despite Mari's constant reminders to wait until she was fully recovered, Astrid couldn't help but yearn for the prince's embrace.

With a racing heart and shaky hands, Astrid finally mustered up the courage to push open the door to the prince's chambers. Her eyes scanned the room, searching for her beloved prince.

But instead of the warm and welcoming atmosphere she had expected, a wave of horror washed over her.

There, on the prince's bed, was Flora, the king's ex-bed slave. She knelt on all fours as the prince pounded into her from behind, his hands gripping her plush hips. Her large breasts jiggled with each thrust, her skin slick with sweat.

The dim light of the room flickered, casting a sinister glow over the scene.

Astrid stood motionless in shock, watching the two of them together. The prince's eyes were closed in pleasure as he continued to use Flora, grunting with each thrust.

"Yes," he huffed. "I'm gonna fill up your hole all night."

"Please, your highness," Flora cried out. "Fuck me harder."

Astrid wanted to yell at the prince or push him off of Flora, but her body felt heavy and she couldn't utter a sound.

She stumbled out of the prince's chambers, tears streaming down her face.

Her heart felt like it had been torn into a million pieces.

When she finally made it to Mari's room, she collapsed onto the bed, sobbing uncontrollably. Mari put a comforting arm around her, holding her close.

"There, there," Mari said softly, "don't cry, silly girl. He's just doing what his body tells him to."

Astrid shook her head, unable to stop the tears from flowing. "But I love him," she said between sobs. "I thought that he would only love me too."

Mari sighed. "I know you do, dear, but he's the prince. He needs other women to help him with his needs."

Astrid nodded, knowing that Mari was right, but it was still too much to bear. She clung to Mari, hoping that the older woman's embrace could ease her pain, but it didn't.

As Astrid's physical wounds healed, she returned to her duties as a slave in the palace. She silently cleaned the halls and rooms, doing her best to avoid running into the prince or Flora. She kept her head down and focused on her work, hoping that with time, the pain in her heart would fade away.

She assumed the prince had completely forgotten about her when his arms suddenly embraced her from behind. His warm hands spanned across her stomach, pulling her close until she felt his pelvis pressing against her ass.

Astrid stiffened as his warm breath brushed her neck. She froze, unable to move or push him away.

"What's wrong?" The prince asked.

Astrid tightly gripped the broom in her hand. "I saw you," she choked out. "Sleeping with that other slave."

"What about her?" he asked.

Astrid's eyes narrowed as she tried to keep her voice steady. "You were sleeping with her while I was recovering from giving birth to your children."

"I just needed a release," he laughed. "I didn't want to bother you while you were still recovering."

Astrid's heart dropped. She couldn't believe the callousness of his words. "I thought you cared about me," she said, her voice barely above a whisper.

"I do care about you. But I have needs too." He pulled her close, the pulsating heat of his arousal pressing against her lower back. "I miss being inside you."

Astrid pulled away from him, hurt and anger coursing through her veins. She had given everything to the prince, but he didn't seem to care.

"Why are you acting like this?" He asked. "Isn't your task to help me cum?"

Astrid wrenched her arm away from him and ran down the hall, tears streaming down her face.

Flora was right. She was just a toy to him, a warm hole to play with when he wanted to fuck.

Astrid felt foolish for believing that the prince cared about her.

*　*　*

Astrid knocked on Forest's door.

"Come in!" said his muffled voice from inside.

Astrid pushed the door open. The room was dimly lit. The air was thick with the scent of opium.

Forest was slumped against the bed, eyes half-closed, breaths coming slowly and evenly.

"Astrid," he murmured, a hint of surprise in his voice.

Astrid stepped inside. She wasn't sure why she was there. All she wanted was to spend time with someone who was as angry and hurt as her.

Forest held out his pipe. "Want some?"

Astrid hesitated for a moment before taking it. She swore never to smoke opium, but she wanted to forget about the prince, if only for a little while.

She coughed as she took her first drag of the pipe. It had a sweet, almost fruity taste and a subtle earthy aroma.

"It sucks, doesn't it?" said Forest. "To have no control."

"It's better than being on the homeworld."

"Do you seriously believe that shit about Earth being a living Hell?"

"But it's the truth."

"If things were better there, do you think they'd tell you. They want you to think that it's an honor to be used as a monster's fuck toy."

Astrid huffed and took another drag of the pipe. All conversations with Forest quickly turned to his hatred of their masters.

Forest took the pipe from Astrid. "Back when I was a breeder, they'd put the women to sleep and make us fuck them that way. All quiet and still so they wouldn't fight back. Some of them begged us not to do it, but we didn't have a choice. It was so fucked up."

Astrid usually blocked out Forest's crazed rantings, but after her experience with the prince, she couldn't help but agree.

"That isn't the way that things are supposed to be," said Forest.

"Yeah, maybe not," Astrid muttered, taking back the pipe.

Warmth spread through her body as she continued to smoke. All her cares and worries slipped away.

Astrid understood how so many slaves became addicted.

Forest watched with a mixture of concern and fascination.

"I missed you," he said softly.

Astrid felt a pang of guilt, but she couldn't deny the thrill she felt at his words.

"I missed you too," she whispered.

Astrid leaned in closer, heart pounding as she closed her eyes and pressed her lips to Forest's.

At first, he was hesitant, but then he responded, lips parting as he deepened the kiss.

Astrid ran her fingers through his hair, pulling him closer as he wrapped his arms around her, holding her tightly.

Their kiss was slow and gentle, a delicate dance of lips and tongues that left them both dizzy and breathless.

Forest's hands moved to her waist, pulling Astrid onto his lap as he sucked her lower lip. His hands moved up and down her back, caressing her curves as she melted into him.

The need and desire grew until it was almost unbearable. Astrid rocked against his groin as he hardened beneath her.

Forest moaned, thrusting his hips up against Astrid as he matched her rhythm.

Astrid pulled away, breathing heavy and cheeks flushed. She lifted up her dress and lowered herself onto his cock, sighing in pleasure as he filled her completely.

It wasn't what she wanted, but it was enough. She'd use Forest to fill the gaping hole inside her.

Forest hissed as he disappeared into her wet warmth. His hands moved down to her hips as he thrust upwards, pushing himself further into her depths.

Astrid shuddered as she was hit by the first wave of sensation. She rubbed her swollen clit against his pulsing dick with every rock of her hips.

Forest's breathing was ragged as he threw back his head, swearing under his breath as he tried to hold back his orgasm.

Astrid gasped, nails digging into his shoulders as she rode him faster and harder, using his body to distract herself from her own pain.

The pleasure built up inside until it was too much to bear. She bit her lip and let out a cry as she came, shaking in his arms as he tensed beneath her. Fire danced along her nerves, igniting her blood with every beat.

Forest joined her in ecstasy.

His hands clasped Astrid's hips, fingers sinking into her skin as he drove himself further. His face contorted with pleasure as his teeth clenched.

Her name was on his lips with each thrust, punctuating the wet sounds of their bodies joining together. In one final movement of bliss, he spilled himself inside Astrid. The warm heat of his release filling her.

Astrid collapsed against Forest's chest, body still trembling from the intensity of the climax.

Forest kissed the top of her head as they sat together in silence. The warmth and pleasure slowly faded away.

Astrid didn't care what the prince thought anymore. He never belonged to her to start with. She was just a play thing in his rapidly growing collection.

Astrid would fuck whoever she wanted.

The prince left Astrid alone. As her master he could call on her at any time to spred her legs, but he busied himself with his other new bed slaves.

There were at least three young women who took turns sharing his bed.

"He's so demanding," Astrid overheard a curvy blonde woman laughing with her friend. "Look at these claw marks on my hips."

"That expanding dick was a shock at first," replied a tall brunette who was pregnant with another slave's child. "But I've come to kind of like it."

"I can see why that thin bitch dug her claws in and refused to let go."

Astrid pretended that none of them bothered her. She spent years as a lowly slave who washed the floors. She had no problem returning to a quiet existence.

Astrid was on her hands and knees, scrubbing the stone floor of the kitchen when Mari appeared. Astrid straightened up, wiping the sweat from her forehead as Mari's serious expression caught her attention.

"Astrid, you've been summoned by the king." Mari's voice was low and urgent.

"What?" Astrid said, assuming that she had misheard.

"The king has summoned you," said Mari. "You are to go to his rooms."

Astrid froze as the meaning of those words slowly sunk in.

"But why?" Astrid asked. "Why me?"

"Who knows. But you know what the king's orders mean."

Astrid nodded and put down her brush.

Mari took her by the arm and led her out of the kitchen, through the palace halls, and into a luxurious room filled with perfumed steam.

Astrid sat nervously on a plush cushion while a group of slaves worked to prepare her for the king's summons.

"It's best to think of this as….a new opportunity," said Mari. "A place in the king's bed is one of the most desired in the palace."

"Is he rough?" Astrid asked.

"Perhaps… if he becomes too excited. But many of his bed slaves brag about his generosity."

Astrid clenched her hands into fists. She spent months in his son's bed. Fucking the king couldn't be too different.

Slaves bustled around Astrid, painting her face and carefully arranging her hair. They selected a revealing gown for her to wear.

The dress had a low-cut neckline that left little to the imagination and exposed much of Astrid's legs. It was made of a soft, shimmering fabric that clung to her curves, emphasizing every inch of her figure.

Astrid sat silently, heart pounding, as they finished their work.

Astrid sat on the edge of the king's bed.

The room was full of opulence, every inch dripping with gold, silver, and jewels. The walls were adorned with rich tapestries, depicting scenes of epic battles and royal banquets. The bed was carved from the finest wood and draped in silken sheets. A canopy of velvet hung above it, framing the bed like a regal crown.

Astrid couldn't help but marvel at the sheer luxury of it all. She had never seen such extravagance before, not even in the prince's chambers. Everything in the room seemed to gleam.

Astrid sighed and looked down at her hands.

She wondered what the king wanted. Would he be gentle and kind, or demanding and forceful? The uncertainty made her heart race.

Astrid jumped as the door slammed open and the king entered.

He was a monstrous wolf with sleek black fur. He towered over her, easily twice her height. Thick muscles rippled under his fur, and his yellow piercing eyes looked down at her with a hunger that made her heart skip.

He was a monster who had conquered worlds and taken countless females to his bed.

Astrid couldn't help but feel a twinge of fear mixed with desire as he closed in on her.

"So this is the human who gave birth to my son's pups?" he said.

The king's voice was deep and rumbling, like thunder in the distance. His sharp teeth gleamed as he spoke.

"Yes, your majesty," Astrid replied, voice barely above a whisper.

The king studied her for a moment, eyes scanning over her body.

Astrid felt exposed in her revealing gown, breasts swollen with milk. She averted her gaze, feeling a blush rise to her cheeks.

"You are quite beautiful for a human," the king said, voice almost a growl. "I can see why my son was so taken with you."

Astrid felt a pang of guilt as she thought of the prince.

"Thank you, your majesty," she said quietly.

The king stepped closer, his large paw-like hand reaching out to stroke her cheek. Astrid flinched, but he only chuckled.

"No need to be afraid," he said. "I will treat you well, as long as you obey."

Astrid nodded, feeling a sense of resignation wash over her.

"Lay back," he said. "I want to examine you."

Astrid did as he commanded, hesitantly laying back on the soft sheets.

The king climbed up onto the bed, his powerful frame towering over her smaller form. He studied her body with an intense gaze, his eyes tracing the curves of her figure.

Astrid felt a shiver run down her spine as the king's rough hand grazed her thigh. She was both frightened and aroused by his touch.

"What do you want from me?" she asked.

The king leaned in closer, hot breath caressing her neck. "I want to know what it feels like to fuck the hole that birthed my grandchildren," he growled. "I want to feel my son's favorite whore tremble around my cock."

Astrid gasped as the king's lips brushed her skin, sending a jolt of desire through her.

If she closed her eyes, then she could pretend that it was the prince.

The king moved his large hands down her body, ripping away the thin fabric of her dress. Astrid gasped as he exposed her body to the cool night air, her nipples hardening at his touch.

The king ran his tongue over her skin, licking and exploring every inch. His hands roamed hungrily all over her body, teasing and caressing her in ways that sent waves of sensation coursing through her veins, making it difficult for Astrid to think straight. His hardness pressed against her leg.

Astrid held her breath as the king slid his hands along her thighs, parting them gently.

His mouth moved between her legs, licking her dripping slit. His tongue was like fire, circling her clit and sending waves of joy radiating through her core. His fingers delicately teased and caressed her sensitive nub.

Every nerve in Astrid's body thrummed in anticipation as intoxicating pressure built within her.

She shuddered and moaned beneath him, clasping the sheets.

The king grinned as his tongue explored deeper, probing every nook and cranny of Astrid's most intimate area. He lapped at her with passionate vigor, teasing and stimulating. His rough tongue played an exquisite symphony that sent desire coursing through her veins until she felt like she was going to explode.

Astrid felt a hot, tingling sensation slowly growing in her belly, radiating outward until it engulfed her whole body. The pressure intensified with each second, becoming almost unbearable before cresting in one powerful wave that made her gasp and cry out in bliss.

The king let out a satisfied hum. He pulled away and climbed up her body. His hard muscular chest pressed against her.

"You belong under me now," he whispered, breath hot against her ear. His swollen erection pressed against her thigh.

Astrid knew that there was no escape from the king's grasp. She was his to do with as he pleased. As frightening as the thought was, it also filled her with a heady sense of excitement.

She closed her eyes and leaned into him, her lips softly brushing his. His hands slid up the back of her neck and he kissed her deeply, exploring her mouth with his tongue.

For a few blissful moments, Astrid forgot about everything else, lost in the heat of the moment.

The king's hard length thrust forward, pushing aside her slick walls and brushing against her inner core.

She gasped loudly and her body quivered with anticipation as his thick shaft filled her completely, stretching and massaging her from within. Her breath grew heavier with each thrust. She arched her back in pleasure, feeling his velvety cock slide deeper and deeper.

"On your hands and knees," the king hummed and pulled away.

Astrid complied. She trembled as the king moved closer and positioned himself behind her. His hands roamed across her curves, leaving trails of warmth in their wake.

She could feel his hard arousal against her backside and gasped as he slowly pushed in. Pleasure surged through her, each thrust sending ripples of delight through her entire being and making every inch of her inner walls come alive.

The king thrust with more force, each stroke sending sparks through Astrid. The sensation was exquisite.

She felt herself growing wetter as his body moved against hers. Astrid gasped as pressure built up within her again, and he increased his pace, pushing into her faster and faster until she was screaming.

The king's muscles tensed and tightened with each thrust. His eyes closed and his face was a mask of sheer bliss.

"All human females need the same thing," the king groaned. "A thick cock and warm seed to fill them up."

"Yes," Astrid huffed as he pounded her pussy. "Yes, your highness."

The wet sounds of their skin slapping together was like music to her ears.

"You feel so good, your highness," Astrid moaned, deciding to humor him. "So thick and powerful…"

The king's lust-filled eyes rolled back as his appendage stirred within Astrid.

She felt hot tension building between them as his manhood swelled within her, stretching her sheath to its limits.

His hot seed spilled out in an eruption that sent a tremor through both their bodies, filling her with warmth.

Astrid's pleasured moans reverberated in the room as a wave of heat coursed through her body, stronger than any flame she had ever experienced before. Her muscles tightened and her toes curled as her climax reached its peak.

Pure joy exploded outwards from her groin.

"Good girl," the king hummed, trailing his fingers down her back as he continued to pump his seed deep inside her. "So warm and tight like a good cock slave."

Astrid lay panting, feeling both relieved and disappointed that they had finished.

She could feel the stirrings of something new inside of her. Something that she had never felt before.

The need to use someone to advance her own position.

"Thank you, your highness," Astrid smiled back. "You are so wonderfully....handsome and talented."

Chapter 7

"You're so big, your highness," Astrid groaned as the king's throbbing erection pounded deep inside her. "So fertile and strong."

The king's thick shaft plundered the depths of her passage as he thrust in and out with deep grunts, eyes closed and head thrown back.

Astrid ran her hands over his large upper arms, feeling the ripple of hard-packed muscle and the warmth of his body. His fur was like plush velvet beneath her fingers, thick and dense, its scent sweet and musky.

They were sitting on his bed, legs wrapped around each other's waists as he slowly rocked inside her.

She watched his throbbing dick move in and out with each thrust. Just the sight was enough to make Astrid tense and shudder.

She was fully naked, breasts swollen and dripping with milk. The king's rough tongue lapped up the white liquid that spilled out and ran down her pale skin.

Astrid gasped and let out a moan as the king sucked on a hardened nipple, his large tongue working around it. He released her breast and kissed her hungrily, lips insistent and rough against her own as he continued to rock inside her.

Astrid closed her eyes and let out a whimper as he picked up the pace, pounding into her with a ferocious tenacity that sent waves of pleasure radiating through her core.

Astrid couldn't deny that it was hot to have such a large and powerful being using her to satisfy his monstrous urges.

It made it easier for her to forget about the prince.

"Your cock is so wonderful, your highness," Astrid moaned. She'd quickly learnt that the king loved praise. "I've never felt so good before."

The king let out a low growl. His thrusts grew deeper and more powerful.

"I want to be full of you," Astrid gasped, reaching between her legs to slowly rub her swollen clit. "Breed me.......please."

"You're going to feel every inch," the king groaned. "I'm gonna fill you up."

"Please, your highness," Astrid moaned, inner walls clenching around him. "Please give me all your seed."

The king gripped Astrid's hair and pulled her head back, his great weight pinning her down.

Astrid gasped for breath as he pushed into her with frantic thrusts, hips slapping hard against her as he drove into her quivering flesh.

Astrid's body tensed as intense pressure built up inside her. She dug her nails into the king's shoulders, screaming as he continued to thrust. Her head swam as she clenched her eyes shut.

She felt joy cascading through her as the king's manhood expanded, pushing against her walls and sending ripples of sensation through her body.

Warmth flooded her depths as the king's seed spilled out, filling her to the brim. His large body shuddered.

Astrid's inner walls contracted, her muscles sucking up the king's hot cum.

"Thank you, your highness," Astrid panted. "Thank you for filling me up."

The prince's face flashed across her mind, but she blinked the memory away.

She was with the king now. The prince was insignificant.

The king's mouth curved into a satisfied smirk. He collapsed beside her.

"You're so voluptuous and fertile," the king whispered as he caressed her dripping breasts. "So warm and delicious."

He leaned forward to lap the milk from Astrid's chest as his cock continued to pulse inside her.

He moved his finger in a circular motion between her legs, exploring the slick folds and finding her engorged clit. He massaged it gently, eliciting a gasp from her lips.

Astrid moaned and writhed underneath him, the sensations too intense for her to bear. His lips and tongue delicately teased her nipples, drawing out more of the milky liquid that dripped down her skin.

The king groaned as his hands roamed her curves, exploring every inch of her flesh with a mixture of passion and hunger.

Astrid felt as if she was about to burst as the king's tongue continued to drive her wild.

She let out a loud moan and pressed herself against his face, pushing her breasts further into his mouth as he sucked hungrily.

She lost all sense of time, blissfully unaware of anything else but the warmth and pleasure that surrounded them both.

The king expertly moved between kissing and sucking on Astrid's nipples while rubbing her clit, creating delicious pressure between her legs.

Her inner walls clenched around him, squeezing tight in delight as a powerful orgasm gripped her entire body like an electric shockwave. She let out a loud cry of ecstasy as liquid heat flooded from between her legs.

The king groaned with delight.

"You're so skilled, your highness," Astrid moaned as the king's thick cock pressed deep inside her. "So smart and talented in bed."

"Mmmm," the king hummed into her ear, pumping his hips with deep strokes that pushed his seed deeper inside. "You're not shy at all."

Astrid gripped his thick fur as her head fell against the pillows, back arching off the bed as the king thrust.

He had a short refraction period from fucking multiple women a day. It wasn't strange for him to be quickly hard and ready again. His ancestors were famous for having multiple wives and hundreds of children.

The king's rhythm quickened, selfishly using her warm heat to satisfy his inhuman needs.

Astrid was too spent to match his pace. She lay back and let him take what he wanted.

Her body shook as he slammed into her, his thick swollen member massaging her inner walls. She groaned out of habit, voice rising in pitch as the king fucked her harder and faster.

He cried out as his body jerked one last time, spilling himself deeply into her depths until she was completely filled with his essence.

The king's manhood continued to softly pulse inside her as warm cum spilled out, drenching the sheets beneath them.

"Good girl," the king hummed, running a hand through Astrid's hair. "At least all that time spent with my stupid son made you good at taking cock."

Astrid walked confidently into the king's harem, head held high despite the fluid still running down her bare thighs.

There were several large and curvaceous women lying around dressed in expensive silk and jewels. The king liked his human women bigger, so they were provided with rich foods instead of the bland gruel given to the other slaves.

Several women glanced at Astrid with envy while pretending not to care. They all knew that their position was temporary. The king would discard them once he lost interest.

Astrid didn't give a shit about the future. She planned on enjoying all the benefits while she still had the chance. All she needed to do was look pretty while lying around gorging herself on food and wine. There was no need to clean floors or wait on any royal. It was the easiest job that she'd had in her life.

Astrid walked over to her assigned cushion, taking a seat as several slaves rushed over to clean her up. The king wouldn't call upon her again so soon, but she needed to look presentable and ready at all times.

"For you," said one young girl as she passed Astrid a bowl of fruit. "The king has requested that you gain more weight."

Astrid nodded and took a bright fruit, digging into it with vigour as the flavours exploded against her tongue.

She'd happily fuck the king a thousand times for the chance to eat such delicious foods.

"Maybe he chose her because she's such an animal," whispered a large bed slave behind Astrid.

"He brags about drinking her milk," said another. "It's like fucking a cow."

"I do hope that he doesn't expect such disgusting acts from the rest of us."

Astrid silently chewed while trying to ignore them. She told herself that they'd be gone soon enough. No slave lasted more than five years in the king's harem.

❄ ❄ ❄

Astrid's new room was just large enough to fit a sleeping mat and blankets. She could usually ignore the sobbing from the girl who slept in the next room.

It was better than the cramped dorms and cold closets that she'd been forced to sleep in until then.

It also gave the prince the confidence to visit her.

Astrid was awoken by the sound of the wolf royal sliding open her bedroom door.

His large feet padded against the stone floor, silently moving closer until he was standing right next to her sleeping mat.

He reached out and brushed his clawed fingers against her cheek.

"Astrid," the prince whispered softly. He bent down and kissed her forehead tenderly before whispering in her ear. "I miss you so much."

Astrid didn't reply. What was there to say? He was her master. She couldn't express her real feelings without fear of being sent away, so she remained silent.

The prince smiled sadly and ran his hand down her back, tracing the curve of her spine with a gentle caress. His touch was soft and tender.

Astrid almost forgot the world around them.

Almost.

He stopped when he reached her lower back and began to massage it gently, kneading the tense muscles until they softened beneath his fingertips.

He leaned in closer until his breath tickled her earlobe. "Please let me inside you."

Astrid stiffened. She wanted him to leave, but she also missed his touch.

Astrid shuffled over, silently giving him permission.

The prince pulled back the blankets and gently slipped beside her, his hand stroking Astrid's hair as she lay facing away from him. He pulled up her nightdress, exposing her naked ass.

The prince moved closer until his body was flush against hers. He slowly slipped inside, pushing himself deep into her warm depths with a hiss of pleasure.

Astrid clenched her teeth to suppress a groan.

The prince started to move, thrusting in and out at a slow steady pace as Astrid buried her face in the pillow.

It was hard to feel mad with his warm body pressed against hers. It felt like he was melting into her.

Astrid quivered beneath him as he continued to stroke and thrust.

The prince's pace quickened, moving at a frenzied desperate rhythm as his body tightened. He pumped faster, harder, deeper, as he grew closer and closer to orgasm.

Astrid clamped down around him, her tight walls milking every drop of pleasure from his dick.

The prince released a long drawn out moan as his climax hit at full force, hot cum spraying from his dick. His body trembled as waves of pleasure washed over him, lingering for moments before slowly dissipating.

He lay panting, still connected to Astrid, cum flowing deep inside her.

She resisted the urge to slip a hand between her thighs.

He stayed there, hugging her tightly, until his heart rate returned to normal.

He gently pulled out. White fluid flowed out of her body and onto the sheets, pooling beneath them both.

The prince rose from the bed, hesitating for one moment, then silently left the room, leaving Astrid alone in the darkness.

* * *

"Come." The king beckoned Astrid to the small feast laid out on the table before them. "Sit with me."

Astrid's mouth watered as she eyed the table adorned with an array of exotic dishes from nearby planets. The centerpiece was a platter of succulent meat, its aroma wafting through the air. Alongside it were several bowls filled with steaming fragrant vegetables.

The king patted his lap.

Astrid hesitantly approached, taking a seat on top of his warm thighs.

The king drew her close and tucked her against his strong chest. His heavy arm draped around her frame and he nuzzled his face in her hair, breathing in her scent.

"Go ahead," he whispered. "Gorge yourself."

Astrid's eyes lit up when she was presented with a large succulent chunk of meat. Without hesitation, she picked it up in both hands and ravenously tore in, juices dripping from her lips as she savored every bite.

She knew that her lack of manners and grace were obvious, but the king didn't seem to care.

He rolled his groin against her rear, growing larger and harder as she continued to stuff her face.

"That's it," he said with a low hum. "Eat it all."

Astrid nodded, licking her fingers as his throbbing erection pressed against her behind.

He pushed Astrid forward, pulling up her short dress, then slowly sliding himself between her legs, every inch of him disappearing into her wet heat until he was fully engulfed in her embrace. He bottomed out with a groan.

"That's it," he hummed as his thick cock twitched and pulsed. "Keep going."

Astrid continued to eat, even as the king slowly rolled his hips. His strong hands held her firmly in place while his cock teased her insides.

Astrid's chest heaved as she gracefully took him in, the taste of the meat barely registering as she was swept away by the sensations pulsing in her core.

"You're so generous, your highness," Astrid hissed with a subtle roll of her hips. "You give me so much."

The king's face was a mask of raw pleasure as he growled, his eyes closed in bliss as he shuddered.

Astrid moaned and cried out as he began to thrust faster. Her tight walls squeezed his cock, milking him for all he had to give.

His strong hands held her firmly in place as his thick dick slammed against her cervix with each thrust, sending waves of pleasure coursing through her body.

The king pressed his face against her neck and growled as he emptied himself inside her. His face contorted with emotion, his eyes wild and his mouth open in a silent scream of euphoria.

Every inch of his swollen cock brought a wave of pleasure, each new sensation building on top of the last, until Astrid's body was overwhelmed with an electric current that surged through her.

She reached her peak.

Astrid's body quaked and her thoughts blurred as she orgasmed.

The king's strong arms enveloped her as powerful waves of bliss rushed through their bodies, making it impossible to think.

Finally, when it was over, they clung to each other in exhaustion, bathed in the warm afterglow of their shared ecstasy.

"That's a good girl," the king said with a deep rumble of approval. "Now clean your plate."

Astrid did as he commanded, eagerly devouring the rest of the meal as his cock remained firmly lodged inside her.

"This body of yours did an excellent job of growing my grandchildren," the king hummed. One large hand slipped under her dress to cup a breast, the other reached between Astrid's legs to gently tease her clit. "I think that I have another task for you."

Astrid gasped and shuddered beneath his touch. "What is it, your highness?"

"I think that I'll impregnate you."

Astrid failed to hold back a laugh. He couldn't be serious.

"But your highness," Astrid gasped as his thick fingers brought her groin back to life. "You already have a son."

"I have a runt," the king laughed, running his rough tongue along Astrid's neck. "A weak fool who will run this empire into the ground. Why not use the rest of Lady Rihna's eggs to create more superior heirs?"

A cold chill ran down Astrid's neck as she realized that he was serious.

The king's powerful hands squeezed Astrid's full breasts, kneading them as he pushed up into her.

She gasped as heat and wetness pooled between them.

"This body will grow my new children," the king groaned. "Strong wolves who will lead this empire to glory."

Astrid was too stunned to move, but she couldn't prevent the all consuming orgasm that crashed into her. Every muscle in her body tensed and released as she cried out, each wave bigger than the last.

The king kept thrusting, powerful hips driving into her as he reached his own climax.

"I didn't say that you could stop eating," he huffed. "You need to be nice and fat to nurture my offspring."

CHAPTER 8

"You want it, don't you?" the king huffed as his engorged cock pounded into Astrid's warm depths. "You want me to fill you full of my pups."

"Yes," Astrid huffed as she wrapped her naked legs around the king's thick waist. "Give me babies, your highness."

"How many?"

"So many," Astrid hissed, nails digging into his furry shoulders. "I want to be big enough to burst."

The words were more routine than her own desire, but they managed to excite the king further.

The arm he'd been using to hold her against his chest, suddenly wrapped around her throat and pressed hard against her windpipe in a chokehold.

"You want to be big," he huffed as his hips pistoned in and out. "I'll make you big."

Astrid's breathing grew shallow under the king's crushing onslaught. The air in the room grew thin.

She gasped and clawed at his arms, but he didn't let up.

His pelvis slammed against her clit and his cock rammed into her depths. It was only a minute before she burst into a spectacular orgasm.

Her nails dug into the king's skin as her legs clamped around his hips.

The king growled and released her throat.

Astrid gasped, body convulsing as the orgasm swamped her body. Every nerve tingling in exquisite joy.

The king's grip on her hips tightened as his body began to shake. His hips drove forward one final time, pushing deep into her as his monstrous cock expanded. He let out a guttural roar, sending a flood of warmth radiating from her core as his hot seed filled her up.

Heat radiated through Astrid's body with each wave of pleasure, penetrating to the depths of her being.

It was all fucked up but she didn't care. At least a nice orgasm would distract Astrid from her own thoughts.

The doctor coughed behind the thin curtain.

Astrid and the king came to the medical room for an examination, but the moment that Astrid stripped her clothes, the king decided that he needed to shove himself deep inside her before the doctor could proceed.

"Good girl," the king hummed with gentle thrusts of his hips, emptying out his remaining cum.

Astrid gasped as he pushed her back against the cold metal of the examination table. His hands roamed over her curves, drawing a moan from her lips as he leaned down to suck on one breast. The sensation sent sparks through her body.

She was larger thanks to the excess of food. The king seemed to relish in her increased size, gripping and kneading her soft skin.

He looked up at Astrid with heavy-lidded eyes. A satisfied smirk tugging at the corner of his mouth. A growl rose from his throat as he savoured the flavor of her milk.

Astrid felt his heart beating rapidly as she waited for him to finish.

After what seemed like a lifetime, the king finally pulled himself off, tucking his limp cock back inside his armor as white fluid ran down Astrids legs and onto the floor.

"Enter," the king barked.

A large wolf doctor entered the room, unfazed by Astrid's nakedness and the mess of cum before him.

Astrid spread her legs out of habit, remembering the countless checks that she was subjected to while pregnant with the prince's young.

"Seven of the embryos have matured quite nicely," said the doctor. "We can implant them as soon as the host is ready."

"Good." The king crossed his thick arms over his chest. "I want it done as soon as possible."

The doctor nodded, picking up a thick white scanning rod and inserting it into Astrid's dripping passage.

She let out a hiss of discomfort, but the doctor didn't flinch, inserting it further until it was pressed against her cervix.

He scanned the results on the screen, letting out a nervous hum.

"This one is currently carrying," said the doctor.

"She's what?" The king snapped.

"She…she appears to be a few months along," the doctor nervously stuttered. "You know what humans are like….always jumping on each other after dark…"

The king growled, snapping several orders at the doctor, but Astrid was too focused on the screen to pay any attention.

She was pregnant.

For one short moment she thought that the king could have somehow impregnated her with his seed, but the screen displayed a very human looking fetus.

But there was no way that she could possibly be pregnant with a human child. Unless....

A chair clattered against the floor as the king stormed out of the room.

The doctor let out a sigh of relief.

"I'll prepare the abortion medicine," he said while pulling the rod from her body. "After you drink it, you'll bleed heavily for a week, but once the blood finishes we can prepare you for the implantation with the new embryos."

Astrid nodded, too overwhelmed to say anything.

"You can go," he said with a wave of his hand. "We'll send it to your room."

Astrid's heart pounded in her chest as she stumbled down the palace halls. Her hand unconsciously rubbed the small bump on her belly. She had been feeling strange and unwell for weeks, but she never imagined that she was carrying Forest's child.

Forest.

Astrid clenched her fists, nails digging into her palms as she made her way to the greenhouse.

When she arrived, her eyes immediately fell on Forest, shirtless and sweaty, digging holes in the garden. Despite her anger, she couldn't help but notice the way his muscles rippled with every movement.

Astrid quickly pushed those thoughts aside and grabbed a seedling, throwing it straight at him.

"You fucking liar!" she spat.

Forest jumped in surprise, wiping dirt from his arms. "What was that for?" he demanded.

"You're a liar!" Astrid threw another seedling, this time hitting him square in the face. "A horney, sex-obsessed, cruel fucking liar!"

Forest held up his hands in surrender. "What's going on?" he asked, clearly confused.

"Don't act like you don't know," Astrid yelled, voice echoing through the greenhouse. "You lied about being sterilized!"

"I didn't lie!" He dodged another seedling. "They gave me the surgery and everything."

"Then why am I pregnant?"

Forest nervously chuckled. "Maybe it was the king?"

Astrid felt her face flush with anger. "Don't even joke about this shit."

Forest's smile faded. "Well...you're gonna have to go scream at the other men you slept with, because it can't be me."

"But there isn't anyone else...only you."

Forest bit his lip, his expression troubled. "No...
..It can't be possible.....they said that it was impossible."

"It is," Astrid snapped. "The only people I've slept with are you, the king, and the prince."

Forest bit down on his lower lip and let out a nervous chuckle. "I guess this is a good thing, right?"

"No, it's a terrible thing."

"No, no," Forest hastily corrected. "I mean, it's good. I mean...it's a good thing that you'll have a baby and it's a good thing that it will be mine. I never thought that I'd have children again."

Astrid threw her hands up in the air with frustration. Even when he wasn't high, she still found Forest difficult to understand.

"There won't be any baby," she said. "The king wants me to grow his new children, so they'll be getting rid of it soon."

"No." Forest took a step forward, taking hold of Astrid's upper arms. "They can't do that."

"Why not." Astrid's gaze fell to the ground so she wouldn't have to see the hurt on Forest's face. "It's not like a baby would have a future in this place. They'd probably just be sold off soon after they were born..... or sent to work the mines…Maybe things are just better this way."

Forest shook his head. "No...you can't think like that."

"Then how am I supposed to think! This isn't a world for children."

"But we could find one that is."

"What are you talking about?"

"*We could leave*," Forest whispered. "We could go somewhere else together. You, me and this child."

Astrid let out a laugh. "Where? And how?"

"I don't know, but I've heard of places where humans like us can live on their own. Maybe if we search we can find one."

Astrid shook her head. "They'd just catch us. Then maybe send us somewhere worse."

"Worse than being a monster's babymaker?"

Astrid scowled.

"There's no future for you here," said Forest. "You'll die giving birth to his babies. It's not safe for you here anymore."

Astrid knew that Forest was right. She almost died giving birth to the prince's children.

"We'd never get out," she said. "There's no way."

"He'd help you," said Forest.

"Who?"

"The prince." Forest rubbed comforting circles onto Astrid's upper arms. "Everyone knows that he still comes to your bed at night. I'm sure you could convince him to help."

"How?"

"With your body of course. Tell him that you miss him so much and only want to be with him ....Tell him that he needs to get a ship to hide you off planet."

Astrid silently took in his words. "It sounds like you've had a lot of time to think about this."

"Well...it is pretty quiet in here."

"And you would be part of this plan too, I suppose."

"Of course. Tell him that you need a human caretaker in your new home. All we need is a ship, then once we're off planet we can go wherever we want."

Astrid stepped back, pulling out of his grasp. "I need some time to think about this."

"We don't have much time. It needs to be soon."

"I know just.......Leave me alone for a while."

Forest looked at Astrid for a moment, nodding in understanding. "Alright," he said softly. "Just...think about it, okay? We could have a future together, away from all of this shit."

Astrid didn't respond, instead turning and walking away from Forest and the greenhouse.

It was all too much. One moment she was fucking the king, the next she was pregnant with Forest's baby and talking of escape. She needed time to allow her mind to catch up.

A slave came that evening to bring Astrid the abortion medicine. The small green vile sat on the stand by her bed. All she needed to do was drink it, then the child between her and Forest would be no more.

An order from the king was absolute, but Astrid found herself silently staring at the wall.

The life of a slave was cruel and unforgiving, one that would never be fit for the life of a child. But despite her doubts and fears, she couldn't ignore the longing in her heart to have a child of her own.

Memories of the past flooded her mind, the pain of giving up the prince's babies still fresh and raw. She couldn't bear the thought of letting another child go, not when she had the power to protect them.

If they all died trying to escape, then at least she'd die knowing that she did all that she could.

With a deep breath, Astrid resolved to do whatever it took to ensure the safety and survival of the precious life growing inside her.

❄ ❄ ❄

Astrid shivered as she walked the palace halls, draped only in a short dress and scarf. Several slaves raised an eyebrow as she passed, but said nothing.

Astrid stepped forward, steeling herself against any fear or doubts that threatened to overwhelm her. Quietly but confidently, she knocked on the prince's door and waited for an answer.

The seconds ticked by like hours before there was a response, but eventually a soft voice called out "come in!"

With trembling hands, Astrid opened the door and stepped inside.

The prince sat on his bed, illuminated by moonlight streaming through his window. He looked up as Astrid entered, surprise written across his face.

"Astrid?" he whispered breathlessly, as if unsure of what he was seeing.

Astrid stepped forward and placed her hands on either side of his face, gently caressing his cheekbones with her thumbs.

"I miss you," she murmured softly, leaning in to press a gentle kiss to his lips.

The prince's eyes flickered closed as he returned the kiss hungrily, seeking comfort in Astrid's embrace.

She was surprised at how familiar he felt. All her rage towards him washed away with every press of his lips.

Astrid stepped back and slowly undressed, fingers trembling as they moved to untie the knot at the back of her dress. As the fabric fell away, Astrid revealed her naked body beneath.

The prince gasped, eyes dancing across her curves in awe. "So beautiful," he hummed, voice barely above a whisper.

He reached out to brush his fingertips across Astrid's stomach, tracing a path up to cup her face in his hands.

"I missed you so much," Astrid whispered, trying to appear as lovesick and desperate as possible. "I missed having your thick cock fill me up."

"Is that what you want?" The prince tugged her closer, pressing her warm center against his rapidly growing erection. "I'll fill you up real good."

"*Please*," Astrid hissed. Her small hands reached down to rub his thick manhood. "I need you."

The prince grinned. He reached out to cup Astrid's breast, teasing her nipple with his thumb. "Then I'm yours."

He pulled her into another deep kiss, fingers massaging her plush behind. He took the time to enjoy the feeling of Astrid's small hands rubbing his shaft in slow sensuous circles, letting out a low groan.

He lowered himself onto the bed, pulling Astrid along with him so she was straddling his waist.

She ground against him, pleasuring herself as they continued to kiss.

"I want you," she whispered desperately. "I was wrong to push you away."

"No, I was wrong," he growled. "I should have taken better care of you. I shouldn't have left you alone."

"It's all in the past….make me feel good now."

The prince grinned, hands sliding up to Astrid's hips. He lifted her up and settled her down onto his throbbing cock.

Astrid hissed as her body descended onto him, nails clawing into the prince's muscular chest.

He shuddered, wrapping his arms around Astrid's waist and pulling her close. He repositioned her so she was straddling his waist, her breasts hovering over his face.

The prince took a breast into his mouth and sucked it hungrily, eliciting a throaty moan from Astrid. He moved his head up and down, covering her with passionate kisses as he savored the taste of her sweet milk.

"I've always wanted to try it," he hummed, relishing in the sensation of her tight body around him. "It's just as sweet as I imagined."

"Then drink more."

"Won't my father get mad?"

"No, my body will just make more." Astrid rolled her hips around his cock. "This body can feed both of you."

Astrid gasped as the prince moved on to her other breast, kneading it with his strong hands as he sucked and lapped at it hungrily, sending pleasurable sparks through her body.

Astrid ground against him, feeling tingles of pleasure flutter in her stomach.

He released her nipple and gazed at Astrid's face, their eyes meeting in an intense moment of raw emotion before the prince began to thrust into her eagerly.

He flipped Astrid onto her back so she was lying beneath him on the bed, their bodies still joined together in perfect harmony. He began slowly rocking his hips against hers, setting a gentle rhythm that quickly increased in intensity as they both became lost in the pleasure of the moment.

"Tell me," he huffed. "Tell me that you love me more than my father."

"I do." Astrid squeezed her eyes shut as she was hit by an intense wave of pleasure. "I love you more than I will ever love him."

The prince thrust deep inside her and growled, his body trembling as he released into her with one final surge. Astrid let out a moan and clasped her arms around the prince's neck, pulling him close.

She felt the heat of pleasure building up inside her and let out a shuddering cry as her body was consumed by wave after wave of bliss.

The prince's shaft swelled within her and they both crested, riding the wave of sensation together with their bodies as one. Every inch of her was alight as his seed filled her, a warmth radiating through them in an inexhaustible cascade of joy.

The prince thrust his hips forward, body trembling with ecstasy, his hands dug into her flesh, eyes shut tight as he rode out the last shuddering waves of sensation.

He let out a series of small, huffy grunts and moaned. "I love you."

"I know," Astrid said while gripping him tightly. "I know."

They held each other until he was finished, the prince resting his forehead against Astrid's and breathing in her scent.

She felt the heat radiating off his body, his heartbeat thudding steadily against hers.

"Do you love me?" he asked.

"Yes," Astrid said, praying that he wouldn't see through her lie. "Forever."

She closed her eyes, letting out a languid sigh as exhaustion set in.

The prince pressed a soft kiss to her forehead and rested his arms around her protectively. With their bodies still connected, he slowly drifted off, lulled into a peaceful sleep by Astrid's gentle embrace.

Astrid looked up at the ceiling as she ran her fingers through his fur.

She would get what she wanted. No matter what it took.

CHAPTER 9

The king usually called on his bed slaves to attend to him in his chambers, so it was rare for him to spend time in the harem.

Astrid nervously watched the large wolf king sit on a silk cushion in the center of the luxurious room. He was surrounded by several large women who fawned over him, fighting for attention.

They subtly removed layers of clothing, and served him wine, seductively dancing in an attempt to make him choose them for the evening.

The king didn't move. He sipped from a gold goblet and lazily stroked the hair of the bed slave beside him, occasionally brushing her naked breasts.

Astrid watched silently from a corner of the room, hoping that the king wouldn't call her over.

She needed to appear like she had taken the medicine and was currently bleeding. Luckily the king had little interest in women who were menstruating.

The double doors of the harem flew open with a resounding thud, causing a ripple of surprise among the women inside.

The prince emerged from the dimly lit hallway, his broad shoulders tense and his gaze flickering over the room with a mix of curiosity and suspicion.

The air crackled with a potent mix of anticipation and fear as he drew near, his eyes locked onto Astrid with a hard intensity that made her pulse quicken in her throat.

Astrid quickly looked away.

The slaves all fell silent, their eyes shifting nervously from the king to the prince.

"It's about time you showed up," said the king, raising his goblet of wine towards his son.

The prince's jaw clenched. "I was summoned, Father. I had no choice."

Astrid watched the exchange, heart pounding in her chest.

The king's voice was smooth and measured. "My dear son, I have called you here to remind you of something very important. Learning to respect the boundaries of others."

The prince's face darkened. "What are you talking about, Father?"

"You know exactly what I mean," the king replied, a faint smirk playing across his lips. "Your behavior with my bed slaves has been unacceptable. It's time that I taught you to stop touching other people's things."

The prince's fists clenched at his sides. "I have no idea what you're talking about."

"Oh, I think you know," the king said with a chuckle. "There are no secrets in this place."

The prince crossed his arms over his chest, eyes blazing with anger.

"You," said the king, pointing a finger at Astrid. "Come here."

Astrid's heart raced as the king beckoned her closer, his piercing gaze fixated on her. Her palms grew clammy as she approached him, aware of the other bed slaves' envious glares. She struggled to keep her composure.

"Tell me," the king said, voice low and commanding. "Are you happy here?"

Astrid hesitated for a moment, unsure of how to respond. She knew the king was testing her, and any answer other than the one he wanted could have dire consequences.

Gathering her courage, she forced a small smile. "Of course, your highness. Making you happy is what brings me the greatest joy."

The king's expression softened. He leaned back with a satisfied nod. "You see, my son," he said, turning to the prince. "This one understands her place. She knows that happiness lies in pleasing her king."

The prince's jaw tightened.

Astrid could feel the tension in the air.

She cast a quick glance in the prince's direction, her heart aching at the thought of what she was about to do. But she knew that survival in the king's harem depended on playing the game, and playing it well.

The king smiled, pleased with Astrid's response. He leaned forward, his eyes locked on hers. "You know the best way to make me happy, don't you?"

Astrid's heart raced as she nodded in response.

"Then get on your knees," the king ordered.

Without a word, Astrid got on her knees before the king, the other slaves watching in silence.

The king reached out and stroked her hair, the gesture almost tender.

Astrid closed her eyes and let out a shuddering breath as the king's hand moved down to her neck.

She knew what was expected of her and she would do it, for the sake of her own survival as well as for the king's pleasure. She would make him happy, whatever it took.

As the king's hand pushed her head down towards his groin, Astrid gasped, feeling a surge of both fear and arousal.

She closed her eyes and focused on the task at hand, trying to ignore the other slaves giggles and whispers.

She could feel the king's growing arousal beneath the fabric of his pants. She tried to suppress a shudder as she undid his clothes, freeing his bulging erection.

It gleamed in the low light of the room. Its veins were prominent, visible beneath its silky smooth flesh. It pulsed and throbbed as Astrid's delicate fingers moved around it.

Astrid shuddered as a jolt of sensation rocked her core. She wasn't sure if it was arousal or fear.

She clamped her warm mouth around him, trying to hold back a gag as she felt his thickness expand against her tongue. He tasted both salty and sweet.

"Suck it," the king commanded, tone low and full of lust as he thrust into her mouth. "Make me cum, cock slave."

Astrid nodded.

The king grasped her hair and pushed her face down onto his dick, forcing himself deeper into her mouth.

Astrid closed her eyes and let her tongue dance over the length of his shaft.

"Yes, that's it," the king groaned as she licked the tip of his dick. "Just like that."

Astrid felt him shudder with pleasure.

She moaned, not bothering to hide the moisture rapidly growing between her thighs. Her body didn't care that the prince was watching. It was already preparing itself to be fucked senseless by the king's giant manhood.

The door slammed shut as the prince stormed out of the room.

The king let out a laugh and ran his fingers through Astrid's hair. "That's it," he hummed, thrusting up into Astrid's mouth.

"Drink it all down like a good girl."

Astrid nodded, struggling not to choke.

She kept her mouth tightly around him, focusing on the pleasure she could feel radiating from his body. She felt his muscles tense and quiver as he drew closer and closer to orgasm.

Finally, with one last powerful thrust, the king let out a loud groan as he released his load into Astrid's warm waiting mouth.

Her lips were pulled tight around his member, her cheeks flushed as she struggled to keep up with the intensity of his cum.

Her own groin pulsed with need, but she resisted the urge to slip a hand between her thighs.

The king withdrew his dick from between Astrid's lips, his muscles still quivering from the force of his orgasm.

He pulled her up onto his lap, lips brushing against her cheek.

"Such a hungry little slave," he whispered in her ear. "We'll have to do that again next time that you come to my bed."

He reached out and stroked Astrid's hair, running his fingers through her long locks.

"Thank you, your highness," Astrid said. "I'm happy to have pleased you."

The king's large hand brushed her stomach. "Soon," he whispered in her ear. "Soon you'll be giving me an even greater gift."

Astrid forced a smile, heart anxiously beating in her chest. "Of course your highness. I'm so happy that I can serve you."

That evening, Astrid tiptoed through the palace's dimly lit corridors, trying not to attract any attention. She wore a long flowing robe that caressed her curves as she walked. Her hair was hidden by a long scarf.

Her heart raced as she finally reached the prince's door. She hesitated for a moment before knocking softly. When there was no response, she turned the doorknob and slipped inside, closing the door behind her.

The room was dark, but Astrid could see the outline of the prince's bed in the shadows. She made her way towards it, heart heavy with guilt and desire.

The prince was lying on his side, his back towards her.

She placed a gentle hand on his shoulder, but he flinched away.

"Your highness," she whispered. "Please, can we talk?"

The prince sighed heavily but didn't turn to face her.

"I don't want to talk, Astrid," he said, his voice laced with anger and hurt.

Astrid's heart sank, but she pushed on, desperate to make him understand.

"I only did what I did because I had to, for our safety," she pleaded. "But I don't want to be with him. I want to be with you."

The prince finally turned to face her. There was pain and anger in his eyes.

"You liked it," he said bitterly. "I can tell when you like it."

"It was all just an act," she whispered, her voice barely audible. "I was thinking of you the whole time."

"Is that so?" said the prince, crossing his arms over his chest.

She took a deep breath before speaking. "Yes, it is," she said softly. "I didn't want to do it, but the king made me. You know how he is."

The prince let out a bitter laugh. "Yes, I know how he is," he said, voice laced with sarcasm.

"Please, you must believe me. I was only protecting our future. I want to be together so much that it hurts."

The prince sighed. "It doesn't matter what you want. You're his bed slave now, Astrid. Perhaps things are better this way. Perhaps it's better if we no longer speak to each other."

Fuck, thought Astrid. She was supposed to be seducing the prince, not driving him away.

"What if you hid me away," Astrid said. "Off-world somewhere where no one could find me. Then you could come visit, and we can be together whenever you want."

The prince fell silent like he was thinking it over.

"You could even come too," she said without thinking. "We can start a new life, away from all of this."

The prince let out a sigh. "I don't know, Astrid. It's risky. We could get caught, and then what?"

Astrid moved closer to him, taking his hand. "I'll do whatever it takes," she said, looking up into his eyes. "I can't live like this anymore. I can't keep pretending that I'm happy in the harem, when all I want is to be with you."

"I need some time to think," said the prince, rolling on his side to face the wall. "Please leave me alone."

Astrid's heart sank. She stood there for a moment, unsure of what to do. She needed to convince him to help her leave, no matter what it took.

"Astrid," the prince's voice interrupted her thoughts. "I said I need some time to think."

"I know," Astrid replied softly. "But I can't just leave things like this. Please, let me make it up to you."

The prince turned to look at her again, his eyes full of sadness and confusion.

"How?" he asked.

Astrid took a deep breath and stepped closer to him. "Let me show you how much I care. Let me prove to you that I'm sorry and that I want to be with you."

"And how are you going to do that?"

"With my body."

Astrid pulled up her dress to show him her naked groin, slowly moving her hand down between her legs to cup herself. "Let me show you how wet and desperate I am to feel you deep inside me. Let me show you how much I want to cum around your thick cock."

The prince stared at her in awe for a moment, then slowly nodded. "All right. But we have to be careful. We can't let anyone find out about this."

Astrid nodded in agreement. "I understand."

The prince sat up, inhaling deeply as though savoring her scent. His limp cock twitched to attention between his powerful thighs. "I don't know if this is a good idea. But I want to be inside you, Astrid. You're like a drug to me."

Astrid smiled weakly, her heart racing with excitement and fear. She knew that this was a dangerous game they were playing, but she was willing to take the risk.

She pulled off her head scarf and undid the ties of her dress. She felt a rush of excitement as the fabric slid down her body and pooled around her feet.

The prince reached out with one hand, tracing a line down her stomach before pulling her closer to him.

He kissed her deeply, mouth moving in a perfect rhythm, their tongues intertwining as if they were one, hands pressing into the small of her back.

Astrid climbed up onto his lap, pressing her naked center against his growing erection.

The prince moaned as she ground against him, rubbing her pulsing clit against his sensitive skin.

She didn't even need to act.

He reached up and grabbed her breasts, pinching the nipples between his fingers, watching beads of milk form.

The prince growled with delight, leaning forward and pulling a breast into his mouth, gently sucking on it while kneading her plush behind.

Astrid moaned, body shuddering as she ground on top of him.

It was easy to forget that she was using him to obtain her own goals. All she wanted was to rub herself against him until she came hard against his cock.

The prince leaned back, pulling his mouth from her breast.

"I need you," he said. "I need you now."

"Me too," Astrid whispered, voice almost a gasp.

She reached down to take him in her hand. Her soft fingers curled around his throbbing shaft, brushing the damp tip with her thumb.

The prince moaned with the sensation, body shivering with delight as she stroked him.

"Astrid, please," he moaned. "I need to be inside you now."

Astrid moved closer, positioning him at her entrance. She slowly lowered herself onto his member, feeling the delicious fullness of him inside her.

The prince gasped as she began to move her hips in a slow gentle rhythm, gradually increasing the intensity and depth of each thrust.

The sensation was overwhelming, pleasure washing over them with every movement.

Astrid felt like she was flying on wings of pure bliss.

The prince's hands explored her naked skin, fingertips caressing and teasing until both their bodies shuddered with ecstasy.

Astrid wrapped her legs around him, moaning and arching her back as his cock pulsed inside her. She shifted her hips to get as much friction as possible against her needy clit.

She couldn't resist using his large monstrous body to achieve her own pleasure.

The pressure grew with every movement, until it felt like she was going to burst. She clung to the prince's shoulders, burying her face in his fur.

"It's okay," he growled. "Just do it."

Astrid's breathing became shallow and quick with anticipation, her body electric with pleasure. With each twist of her hips, the intensity grew until she was certain she would explode from sheer bliss.

The prince gasped, gripping her closer.

Pressure exploded outwards from her core like a supernova, washing over her in waves, a crescendo of pleasure that left nothing in its wake.

Astrid hugged the prince tightly, rapidly rolling her hips as she worked out the remains of her orgasm on his hard body.

The prince's nails dug into her behind and he let out a low growl, increasing his thrusts as he chased his own pleasure.

His cock expanded, filling Astrid with unparalleled intensity. He thrust deep into her while growling in pleasure, coming closer and closer to the end.

He released a moan as he spilled inside her, spraying wave after wave of cum with every short thrust of his dick.

Astrid couldn't deny that she loved feeling him fill her. She collapsed against his chest, listening to the rapid beating of his heart.

They stayed that way for what felt like an eternity. The prince's arms wrapped tightly around Astrid's body as they basked in the afterglow of their pleasure.

The prince pulled away, running a clawed hand through her hair as he affectionately looked into her eyes.

"Astrid," he said softly. "Don't ever leave me."

She was temporarily lost for words.

She knew at that moment that he did truly love her.

"Never," Astrid said with a shake of her head.

The prince pulled Astrid tightly to his chest, nuzzling her hair.

"I'll find a way," he said. "It might take a while, but my father will grow weaker with age. I promise that I'll take good care of you once I'm king."

He will never let you be king, Astrid thought, but she bit her tongue and pulled away from the prince's embrace.

"I should go," she said softly. "We can't be seen together like this."

The prince nodded. "I know. But before you go, I have something for you."

He reached into the drawer of his nightstand and pulled out a small, ornate box. He opened it to reveal a beautiful necklace made of pearls and rubies, glittering in the dim light.

"Take this," he said, holding it out to her. "I saw it and thought of you."

Astrid's eyes widened in surprise. She took the necklace from the prince's hand and fastened it around her neck, feeling the weight of it against her skin.

"Thank you," she said. "It's beautiful."

The prince smiled at her, a warm, genuine smile that made her heart flutter.

"You're beautiful," he said, reaching out to tuck a strand of hair behind her ear.

Astrid's heart skipped a beat at his touch.

How could she leave him when he seemed to care so deeply about her?

"I have to go," Astrid said, standing up from the bed and hastily pulling on her clothes. "Goodnight, your highness."

"Goodnight, Astrid," he said, watching as she made her way to the door. "Be careful."

She nodded and slipped out of the room, closing the door softly behind her.

* * *

"Have you made any progress with the prince?" Forest asked.

He was covered in dirt and grease as he fiddled with a broken engine part. There were several other parts and rusted tools scattered across his narrow room.

Astrid shook her head. "Not yet. He's resistant to the idea of leaving. He says he needs more time."

Forest sighed. "Well, we don't have much time. It won't be long before they realize that you're still pregnant."

"I know," Astrid said, wringing her hands. "I'm doing everything I can, but it's not working."

Forest took her hand and gave it a reassuring squeeze. "I've been doing some work in the hanger, trying to learn more about the ships and how to fly them. Maybe there's another way we can escape."

Astrid squeezed his hand back. "That's a good idea."

Forest leaned in to brush his lips against hers, but Astrid pulled away.

She'd had enough demands on her body from the prince and the king. She didn't want it from Forest as well.

"Not now," Astrid said softly. "I just came to talk."

Forest nodded and tried to hide his disappointment, turning his attention back to the engine part. "What's on your mind?"

Astrid took a deep breath, steeling herself for what she was about to say.

"I saw the prince tonight," she said, watching as Forest's expression darkened. "He gave me this."

She held up the necklace for him to see.

Forest's eyes narrowed. "He's just trying to buy you off. He thinks that he can keep you around by giving you gifts."

Astrid shook her head. "It's not like that. He genuinely cares about me. I can feel it."

Forest snorted. "Yeah, right. He's using you, Astrid. He doesn't care about you. He just wants another nice hole for his dick."

Astrid felt a pang of hurt at his words. She knew that Forest was just trying to protect her, but she couldn't help feeling that he was wrong.

"You don't understand," she said, her voice breaking slightly. "He's different. He's not like the king. I can feel it."

Forest's expression softened as he saw the pain in her eyes. His thumb traced soothing circles on her hand.

"I'm sorry," he said softly. "I just don't want to see you get hurt. I care about you too much."

Astrid looked up at him, her eyes filling with tears. "I know," she said. "It's just….he's still afraid of his father….I don't know if I can convince him to help me leave."

Forest sighed and placed a hand on her shoulder. "Astrid… I believe in you. If anyone can convince him to help, I know that it will be you."

Astrid nodded, wiping the tears from her eyes. "I'll keep trying."

Forest hugged her close. "Please, for our future ….and the baby's."

They stayed like that for a few moments, wrapped up in each other, until Forest pulled away, his eyes shining with determination.

"I'll keep working on the ships," he said. "And you keep trying to convince the prince. But if it comes down to it, we'll have to make a run for it by the end of the month."

Astrid nodded, feeling a sense of resolve settling over her. "I'll speak with the prince again."

Forest nodded. "Please Astrid. You're our best chance of getting out of here."

The next morning Astrid made her way to the bath-house, newfound determination pulsing through her veins. She would do anything to make sure that she, Forest and the baby could escape, even if it meant resorting to desperate measures.

Steamy air enveloped her as she slipped through the door. The sound of water splashing echoed through the room.

She spotted the prince, sitting in one of the larger baths, his fur wet and slick. His head was tilted back, eyes closed like he was lost in thought.

Astrid hesitated for a moment, wondering if she should interrupt him, but she knew that time was running out.

"Astrid." The prince opened his eyes as she approached. "What brings you here?"

Astrid took a deep breath, gathering her courage. "I need to talk to you," she said, voice steady despite the racing of her heart.

The prince smiled, gesturing for her to join him in the bath.

Astrid paused for a moment before stripping her clothes and lowering herself into the water beside him.

"What is it that you want to discuss?" he asked, voice warm and inviting. He wrapped an arm around her back, pulling her to his broad chest.

Astrid took a deep breath, feeling the weight of the world on her shoulders.

"The king wants you dead," she said, watching as the prince's expression shifted from amusement to confusion.

"The king?" he repeated, clearly surprised by her statement. "Why would he want me dead?"

Astrid's heart pounded in her chest, but she forced herself to stay calm.

"I don't know why," she whispered. "But he wants to implant his babies inside me. He wants to replace you with new heirs."

The prince's eyes widened in shock. He paused for a moment, lost for words.

Astrid took advantage of the silence to continue. "He wants his own children from Lady Rihna's eggs. He thinks that they'll be stronger than you."

The prince's grip on her tightened. She could feel the anger radiating off him in waves.

"This is outrageous," he said through gritted teeth. "I won't let him do this to you."

"I'm certain that he's going to have you killed soon," said Astrid. "We have to leave. We have to escape together."

The prince fell silent for a moment, his brow furrowed in thought. "I can't just leave.....I have a responsibility to my people.....I swore an oath."

"Forget the people. Your only responsibility is yourself."

"Then I'll kill him," said the prince.

"No. That's not what I meant-"

"I'll challenge him to a duel. If I win then I will be the new king."

"No, please," Astrid begged. "We should just leave. We can find a ship and-"

"Don't worry." The prince pulled Astrid close. He leaned down to lick her neck. "He'll never touch you again once he's dead."

"Your highness-"

The prince thrust his groin forward, slotting his growing erection between her warm thighs.

"It will be okay," he hummed, rolling his shaft against her center. "You and me can finally live together with our pups. I'll take good care of you for the rest of your life."

He groaned and pressed the tip of his cock to Astrid's entrance, shoving himself inside her with several small thrusts.

Astrid hissed and wrapped her arms around his neck.

"We'll be together," the prince huffed as he gently rocked into her wet heat. "Forever."

Astrid clutched his fur and wrapped her legs around his waist, eyes closed as he pressed her against the side of the bathtub.

His idea was insane, but she couldn't deny how alluring it would be to finally live without the king's influence, to finally live together with the children birthed from her womb.

The prince increased his thrusts, strong arms shaking as he held her hips in place and drove into her.

"Do you want that?" he hummed.

Astrid nodded, gasping as she was hit by a strong wave of pleasure. She wanted it so much that it hurt.

The prince's cock swelled inside her, and with one last thrust, he released a powerful surge of heat that sent them both over the edge.

Astrid cried out, eyes rolling back as a powerful orgasm rushed through her body.

At that moment, Astrid knew that she wanted him to rip the king to shreds.

The prince gasped for breath as his seed continued to fill her. He hugged Astrid close, shuddering every time that his dick unleashed a new wave of cum.

"Don't worry," he said, affectionately nuzzling her head. "Soon nothing will keep us from being together."

Chapter 10

Forest's urgent whispers stirred Astrid from her slumber. She sat up groggily, rubbing her eyes. Forest stood over her bed, his face hidden under a dark scarf and several layers of clothing.

"What's going on?" Astrid mumbled, voice thick with sleep.

"I overheard some of the pilots talking," Forest whispered urgently. "They're getting wasted before the king and prince's duel tomorrow, which means the ships are unguarded. We have a chance to escape."

Astrid's eyes widened, her heart racing at the thought of freedom. But then a voice in the back of her head whispered that it might not be necessary.

"But what about the prince's duel?" she asked, her concern evident. "What if he wins? We can't just leave him behind."

Forest's face twisted in anger.

"Are you kidding me?" he snapped. "You want to stay here and watch the prince get beaten to a pulp?"

"I just don't want to leave him behind." Tears pricked at the corners of Astrid's eyes.

"He's not worth risking our lives for." Forest's voice was filled with frustration. "We have a chance to escape now. We have to take it."

Astrid was torn between her loyalty to the prince and her desire for freedom. She knew that Forest was right, but the thought of leaving the prince behind made her stomach twist in knots.

"I can't leave." Astrid shook her head. "I have to see this through."

"You're being ridiculous!" Forest hissed. "Even if he kills the king, then what? Are you going to stay here and see what kind of ruler he's gonna be? Are you going to be his little queen?"

"Maybe," Astrid said, remembering the prince's promise.

Forest took a deep breath. "Fine," he said, voice cold. "Stay here and watch your boyfriend get ripped to pieces. But I'm leaving, with or without you."

With that, Forest turned on his heel and stalked out of the room.

Astrid watched him go, her heart heavy with guilt and regret, but she believed in the prince.

All he needed to do was win and then all their dreams would come true.

The stadium was massive, its stone walls towering high above the heads of the crowd gathered below. The sound of excited chatter and murmurs filled the air. The large wolves of the planet took their seats on the rows of stone benches that surrounded the central arena. The ground beneath their feet was dusty and hard. The scent of earth and sweat mingled together in the freezing air.

The spectators were a colorful mix of creatures, all there to witness the fight between the king and the prince. Some had the same fur and fangs as the two werewolf leaders, while others had skin that shone like polished metal, or tentacles that writhed like serpents.

Despite their differences, they were all united in their shared desire to witness the battle.

Astrid sat with the other bed slaves in the king's tent, occasionally peering through the fabric at the crowd.

Her stomach twisted into knots of anxiety. She couldn't shake the feeling that something terrible was about to happen.

The king didn't seem bothered by the duel. He merrily drank goblet after goblet of wine, laughing with his bed slaves while running his large hands over their bodies.

"We can't wait to see your victory, your highness," one woman laughed coyly, her eyes twinkling with admiration as she looked up at the king. Her lips were curved into a devilish smile as she lightly ran her hands over his muscular fur-covered arms.

"You can fuck me first after you win," said another as she ran her hands over the king's chest.

"No, me," protested another.

"I'm so wet already!" said another. She spread her legs and reached down to rub her dripping sex. "Just the idea of you being covered in his blood makes me so wet."

"Darlings," rumbled the king. "I'll bring you all to my chambers and fuck you for a week after I win."

His cock was already hard and erect, like the idea of murdering his son turned him on immensely.

He grabbed one slave by the waist and pulled her onto his lap, nestling her back against his chest. His hands roamed up and down her bare body as he slowly but forcefully entered her wet heat. A low hiss escaped his lips, his breathing becoming ragged with pleasure.

"Just a taste," he moaned while squeezing her large breasts. "Just a preview of our celebration."

Astrid shuddered.

Please, she prayed. *Please let the prince win.*

A large looming iron gate at the end of the stadium slowly creaked open. Thousands of people in the stands stood and cheered as the prince emerged from the shadows.

Astrid followed his every move, her heart pounding as he made his way onto the arena floor.

Even she could see the nervousness and apprehension emanating from him.

The prince looked around with a grim determination, his muscles twitching and flexing as he took in the spectacle.

The king pulled out of the bed slave before cumming, rapidly jerking himself off until he climaxed with a groan, spraying his seed all over the naked woman.

She laughed like it was hilarious.

Several slaves rushed forth with towels to clean any remains from the king, wiping his dripping cock clean.

"Time to go take care of my son," the king huffed, shoving his still hard dick into his pants.

He staggered to his feet, the buzz from the wine becoming more than obvious.

Maybe we still have a chance, Astrid thought, nervously clenching her hands.

The air was thick with tension as the king made his grand entrance, fur wild and his eyes ablaze with fury. The crowd erupted into deafening cheers as he stumbled towards the center of the arena, waving his arms and bellowing at the top of his lungs.

Astrid's heart pounded in her chest as she watched the king fix his gaze on the prince, a cruel smile spreading across his snarling face.

"Look at him, my people!" he shouted to the crowd. "This insolent weakling thinks he can take my crown!"

The prince stood tall and defiant, his eyes locked onto the king's as they began to circle each other, muscles taut and ready for battle.

"Today shall be your last day as my son," the king hissed, claws extending menacingly.

"That's because I will become a king," the prince shouted back, voice strong and unwavering.

The king lunged at the prince with a fierce growl, his claws slicing through the air. The prince braced himself for the impact, but the king was too fast, too powerful. He landed a brutal blow to the prince's side, causing him to stumble and fall to the ground.

The crowd cheered as the king mercilessly pummeled the prince, giving him no chance to defend himself. Astrid's heart sank as she watched the prince's grey fur become matted with blood and his eyes glazed over with pain.

In a sudden burst of energy, the prince fought back, landing a powerful punch to the king's jaw that sent him reeling backwards.

Astrid's spirits lifted with hope as she silently cheered for the prince, but it was short-lived. The king quickly regained his composure, returning to savagely beating his son.

A final, devastating blow sent the prince crashing to the ground, his body limp and lifeless.

The crowd went wild, roaring for the king.

Astrid's hands flew to her mouth, tears streaming down her face as she watched in horror.

The king turned to face her, his chest heaving and his eyes wild with power. Astrid trembled under his gaze, unable to meet his bloodshot eyes.

The prince lay motionless on the ground, his breathing shallow and weak. Astrid's heart ached as she watched him, his body broken and battered.

The king let out a triumphant roar and turned to face the crowd, arms raised in victory.

It was over.

The king had won.

Astrid was his to do with as he pleased.

Astrid's mind raced as she tried to make sense of what happened. The weight of her fear and desperation felt like an anchor, dragging her down into a dark abyss.

She stumbled through the empty halls, her feet barely touching the ground as she raced towards Forest's room. Her heart hammered in her chest, threatening to burst through her ribs.

It felt like she was trapped in a nightmare

As she burst into the room, Astrid's hopes were dashed. Forest was nowhere to be found, and the room was eerily silent.

Panic seized her heart as she realized that he had left her.

Tears streamed down her face as she sank to the floor, her sobs echoing through the empty room. The thought of losing Forest was unbearable, and the fear of being alone overwhelmed her.

"Fuck you, Forest!" she cried. "Why couldn't you wait?"

Astrid clutched at her chest, feeling as if her heart would explode.

Without Forest or the prince, she had no one left.

The king towered above her, his massive frame casting a menacing shadow. His eyes were inhumanly bright, and his sharp teeth glinted in the moonlight. She felt like she was facing down a primal force of nature.

"*So disobedient,*" he hissed, bulging muscles rippling with power. *"You've given me no other choice."*

Astrid trembled as the king advanced, her eyes wide with fear.

The rage contorting his face was terrifying to behold, like a monster from nightmares. He grabbed her by the shoulders and shoved her onto the bed, trapping her beneath his giant frame.

She wanted to scream for help, but no sound escaped from her lips. Instead, she lay petrified as the king moved closer.

His hands slid over her curves, exploring every inch of her body in a possessive manner before finally settling between her legs.

Heavy breathing filled the room as he thrust himself inside of her body with a loud groan, his cock bigger than it ever had been before.

He moved with intensity, pushing deep into her body like an animal. His muscles flexed as he continued to thrust, filling her with a mixture of pleasure and pain.

Astrid felt her body responding to him, as if it had a will of its own. She gasped for air as waves of sensation consumed her entire being. She found herself screaming out in ecstasy.

"That's it," the king hissed. *"Let them all know how much you love my cock."*

The king's movements slowed, but his grip on Astrid never loosened. He leaned forward and whispered in her ear. "You belong to me now."

Astrid trembled beneath him, still lost in the throes of passion even as the words filled her with dread.

The king let out a fierce roar as he thrust his muscular hips against her. His claws extended from his fingers, leaving burning marks on her skin as they dug into her back.

The king howled as he increased his speed, shamelessly using Astrid's flesh for his own fucked up pleasure.

He growled and trembled, back arching as he came, pumping Astrid full with wave after wave of hot seed.

It spilled from her body, pooling on the bed below them without any end. He shuddered in ecstasy while tightly clenching her skin.

"Soon," the king groaned as he continued to rock his hips. "Soon you'll give me a new prince."

"Astrid," a soft female voice whispered. *"Astrid."*

Astrid jolted awake, blinking in confusion as she took in her surroundings.

She was in her own room, not the kings.

It was just a dream.

The intoxicated monarch spent the evening celebrating and fucking his favorite slaves.

Astrid took the opportunity to sneak back to her room, anxiously counting down the hours until he would call for her. She drifted off to sleep with her make up still smudged from her tears.

Astrid flinched away as she felt a gentle hand on her shoulder. She turned to see Flora leaning over her bed.

The older woman's red hair was tied back into a bun. She wore a white nightgown that covered most of her pale skin, leaving only her neck and shoulders bare.

"Come on, Astrid," Flora whispered urgently. "You should come see this."

"What is it?" Astrid whispered.

Flora placed a finger to her lips and held out her hand.

Astrid nervously took it and slipped out of bed.

Confused and still groggy, Astrid followed Flora down the dark corridors of the palace. They descended a winding staircase to the basement, where the air was damp and musty. Astrid could hear the sound of her own heartbeat pounding in her ears.

Flora led her to a small room with a flickering torch on the wall. The room was full of dusty garbage, except for a crumpled figure lying on the ground.

Astrid gasped as she recognized the prince.

His beaten up body was a pitiful sight. His face was swollen and bruised. His fur was mattered with blood. It dripped from his nose and split lip, pooling on the floor.

The prince's breathing was labored and shallow. It was a miracle that he was still alive.

Astrid felt a surge of anger and sadness.

"Isn't it wonderful," said Flora as her mouth curved up into a smile. "Now he finally knows what it's like to suffer."

Astrid's brow narrowed in confusion. "What do you mean?"

"I never thought that I'd see him like this. It almost makes up for all the times I had to take his disgusting cock."

"Why are you talking like this? We have to help him."

"Why should we?" laughed Flora. "He's just another fucking monster who used us."

"But he's hurt, we can't leave him here like this," Astrid pleaded. "He might die."

"He's getting what he deserves," Flora hissed. "They use us like animals and then toss us aside when they're done. This whole palace deserves to burn to the ground."

"But he's dying," Astrid protested. "We have to do something."

"Let him die. I want to stand here and watch him take his last breath."

Astrid felt a wave of helplessness wash over her.

She knew that Flora was right. The royals had treated her people like dirt for centuries, but she couldn't stand by and watch the prince die.

She knelt down next to him, gently running her hand through his blood stained fur.

Flora rolled her eyes. "You're still so naive and brainwashed, Astrid, even after all the shit that-"

"Flora!" snapped a stern voice.

Astrid turned to see the head slave, Mari, quickly making her way down the narrow stairs.

"You should not be here!" the old woman snapped. "Speaking such blasphemy against the royal family."

Flora's eyes narrowed, her lips pursed together. She crossed her arms in frustration. Without another word, she spun on her heels and marched down the hallway.

Mari's gaze softened as she approached Astrid. "Astrid, that means you too," she said gently.

Astrid's face went numb as she attempted to hold back her tears. "Please," she begged. "Just one last time"

She held the prince's hand tightly. The thought of leaving him was excruciating.

Mari nervously shifted her weight. "You shouldn't be here, Astrid. The king ordered that he be left alone."

Astrid looked up at Mari with pleading eyes. "Please, just a little longer. I won't cause any trouble. I just want to be here with him."

Mari sighed. "Alright. Just a little longer. But then you must leave, understood?"

Astrid nodded. She turned back to the prince and squeezed his hand. "I'm here," she whispered. "You're not alone."

*   *   *

Astrid sat by the prince's side, her hand resting on his chest as she watched his breathing become shallower with each passing moment. She was barely breathing herself, her heart pounding loudly in her chest.

It felt like they had been there for hours, trapped in a never-ending nightmare.

"How the mighty have fallen," echoed a deep voice from the darkness.

Astrid spun to see Forest emerge, the lines under his eyes deep and pronounced. His gaze settled on the prince's still form.

"Not so handsome now, is he," he sneered.

Tears welled up in Astrid's eyes. "I thought you left," she whispered.

"I did try to," he said, his voice low and gravelly. "But I need the handprint of a wolf to start the ship's engines."

Astrid's heart sank as she realized their chances of escape were fading.

She glanced back at the prince, his breaths growing fainter by the moment.

"So there really is no way to escape," she murmured.

"Not entirely."

Forest's hand moved to his belt. He pulled out a large knife, the glint of steel catching Astrid's eye.

Her heart skipped a beat as she watched him twirl the blade in his hand, his eyes fixed on the prince's wrist.

"We can use his hand to start the engines," said Forest.

Astrid's eyes widened with fear as she watched him approach the prince's body. She wanted to scream, to stop him, but her throat felt tight, and no words came out.

Forest raised the knife, the blade glinting menacingly in the dim light.

"He'll be dead soon anyway," he said coldly. "Might as well make good use of his body while we still have the chance."

Astrid's hand shot out and grabbed his wrist.

"No, Forest," she hissed, tears streaming down her face. "We can't do that."

Forest hesitated for a moment, looking down at her hand on his wrist. "This is our only chance," he hissed. "This is the only way that we can save the baby."

"But not like this."

"Then what else should we fucking do!"

"We could take him with us."

Forest swore under his breath. "He's fucking huge, Astrid. How are we going to get his body all the way to the ship?"

Astrid's mind froze as she struggled to come up with an answer. She glanced at a mound of garbage in the corner of the room.

"There is one way." she said.

The rusty wheels of the garbage cart squealed as they rolled over the stone floor, causing several slaves to turn their heads.

"Fuck," Forest hissed. "This furry arsehole better be worth it."

Astrid's heart pounded as she and Forest pushed the garbage cart through the palace corridors.

The prince, hidden beneath layers of trash, shifted with each bump in the floor.

It was a dangerous plan, but they had no other choice.

The stench of rotting food and waste filled Astrid's nostrils, making her gag, but she kept her head low and moved quickly, hoping to blend in with the other slaves.

Luckily, the other wolves paid them little notice. They were too busy getting intoxicated in the hallways, laughing and fighting as they celebrated the king's victory.

"Fucking psychos," Forest muttered.

Astrid's heart tightened as she watched the other wolves, but she said nothing. All she could think about was the prince, lying unconscious in the cart, his life slowly slipping away.

Was he still breathing?

Was he still alive?

Forest pushed the cart faster as they approached the hanger.

"Hurry!" he snapped.

The expansive hall opened up into a massive cavernous room, the domed ceiling arching far above.

Its surface sparkled in the low light, reflecting the dozen's of sleek ships that lined the smooth runway.

The smell of fuel hung in the air, mixed with a trace of ozone and burnt metal.

"Which ship?" Astrid asked.

"That one," said Forest, leading Astrid to the back of the hanger. "Fuck."

He grabbed Astrid's arm and steered them behind the hull of a sleek golden ship.

"What–" Astrid tried to ask, but Forest silenced her.

A group of wolves came into view. They were huddled around a ship in the middle of the hangar, shouting and cheering as two young wolves grappled with each other.

"Shit," Forest muttered under his breath, his grip on Astrid's arm tightening. "All the ships getting fixed are on the other side of these dickheads."

Astrid's heart sank as she watched them. They looked dangerous and unpredictable.

"Can't we just sneak past them?" she whispered.

Forest shook his head. "They could cause trouble."

The prince groaned, interrupting their conversation. They had to act quickly.

"Come on." Forest pushed the cart back the way that they came. "I have a different idea."

Forest sprinted down the corridor. Astrid trailed closely behind him. They turned a corner, and Forest came to a sudden halt, causing Astrid to almost collide with him.

"No way," Astrid gasped, staring up at the grandest ship in the hangar. It was a breathtaking sight, a solid gold vessel adorned with intricate details that had been carved into its hull. "Is that...?"

"The queen's ship." Forest smiled, nodding his head. "Come on."

They pushed the cart closer to the ship, stopping just before the colossal entrance.

"Help me get this guy's hand against the scanner," Forest instructed Astrid. He threw the garbage from the top of the cart to the ground. "Let's just hope that the queen gives more of a shit about him than his father."

Astrid's heart pounded in her chest as she approached the prince, reaching out to take his warm, bloodied hand. She guided his hand towards the green panel next to the door, pressing it firmly, causing a small light to blink in response.

A low hum filled the air as the panel glowed green, granting them access to the ship.

"It worked," Astrid said, unable to believe her eyes. "The queen really does care."

"Yet she did shit all to help him." Forest pushed the cart into the ship and out of sight before anyone else noticed them.

Astrid followed close behind him, marveling at how grandiose the interior was. The walls were lined with rich fabrics and intricate carvings, and the floors were made of polished marble. It was like nothing she had ever seen before.

"The computer system should be this way," said Forest, leading Astrid down another hallway.

They emerged into a tight, enclosed space filled with intricate buttons, dials and flashing lights. The walls were lined with monitors, some showing various images while others had long scrolling lists of data. In the center was a large chair with a console in front of it, the seat curved to fit a large wolf.

"Here." Forest pointed to a green pad. "We need a handprint here to start the engine."

Astrid nodded.

Together they dragged the prince's battered body from the cart, pressing his hand against the pad.

A low hum filled the air as the engines roared to life.

"We did it," Forest exclaimed as the flight console screen flicked on. "At least he's good for something."

"Do you even know how to fly this thing?" Astrid asked.

"No," Forest admitted while squinting at the screen. "But most of the higher end ships have set coordinates. All we need to do is pick one and go."

Astrid sighed in relief. At least they had a plan. She took a deep breath and tried to steady her shaking hands.

"Okay, let's do this," she said, moving over to the console with Forest.

The screen displayed a list of destinations, each one farther away than the last. Forest scrolled through them quickly, searching for anything familiar. The ship hummed with power, ready to take off at a moment's notice.

"This one," he said, finally selecting a location. "It's far enough away that they won't find us for a while."

Astrid nodded, her eyes fixed on the console as the ship began to lift off the ground.

The ship soared up into the air, its engines blasting a trail of fire behind it as it ascended through the hanger's massive dome. Astrid felt her stomach drop as they shot out of the hanger and into the open sky, the world below them shrinking to a small dot.

Astrid sat in the co-pilot's seat, her heart racing as they soared through the vast emptiness of space. The silence was deafening, broken only by the hum of the engines and the occasional beep from the console.

Astrid took a deep breath, finally allowing herself to relax. The prince lay unconscious in the corner, but she could see the rise and fall of his chest. It gave her some comfort.

They had done it.

"Where are we headed?" Astrid asked, looking over at Forest.

He glanced back at her, a small smile playing at his lips. "Anywhere we can be free."

The orange and pink glow of the setting sun illuminated the vast alien landscape, painting the sky with a mesmerizing array of colors. Astrid gazed at the horizon, taking in the tranquil beauty of the scene before her. The crisp, refreshing air filled her lungs, and she let out a contented sigh.

Five years had passed since they had fled the palace and settled on this planet, but it still felt like yesterday.

"Can I eat these ones, Mama?" Rose's tiny hand thrust a bunch of yellow berries towards Astrid's face.

Astrid examined the berries, turning one over in her hand. "I'm not sure. Maybe Daddy can try one and see."

"Hell no," Forest grunted as he swung his axe into a piece of wood, beads of sweat glistening on his tanned chest. "The last time she brought me some, I had the shits for a week."

Astrid sighed and placed the berries back in Rose's bucket. "Maybe we should leave them for the birds, darling."

"Okay." Rose nodded, skipping away across the fields of purple grass, the bucket bouncing against her side.

She had inherited Astrid's dark hair, which cascaded down her small shoulders, and her eyes sparkled with curiosity and wonder. Astrid couldn't help but smile at the sight of her daughter's expressive face.

As she watched Rose play, Astrid's thoughts turned to the wolf pups she left behind. But raising Rose had given her a new sense of love and purpose. She wouldn't have it any other way.

"I'm going to go out to the woods for a while," said Astrid.

Forest paused for a moment, but didn't say anything. He raised his axe and hacked into the wood with vigor.

Astrid frowned but shrugged it off. She had become used to his silent sulking. Any attempt to get him to open up would be futile.

Astrid grabbed her shawl and set off into the woods, her feet crunching on the fallen leaves as she went.

The thick forest was lush and full of life. Lizard like birds sang in the canopy above her head while small animals scurried away in fear. Astrid was amazed by all the new animals and plants, but couldn't help but feel at home here in this strange land.

Astrid came to a small clearing. At its center was a poorly built cabin. It was small and hastily constructed, with sloppily nailed boards and gaps between the logs. The door was slightly open and soft yellow light streamed out of the cracks.

"You're early," said a low rumbling voice.

The prince emerged from the dense forest, sending shivers down Astrid's spine. She watched in awe as he strode towards her, his once-elegant black fur now matted with twigs and small leaves, giving him a rugged dangerous look.

Despite his imposing size and muscular build, the prince walked with a slight limp, which only added to his charm. There were scars on his face from the fierce duel with the king. A long jagged line ran from his forehead down to his cheek, but it did little to detract from his stunning features.

Nevertheless, the prince exuded an aura of strength and resilience that was impossible to ignore.

Astrid couldn't help but feel drawn to him, no matter how hard she tried to suppress it. There was an unspoken bond between them that only time could strengthen.

"I just wanted to see you," Astrid said softly, moving forward to embrace him.

The prince held her close, his strong arms enveloping her as he buried his face in her hair.

"I missed you," he whispered, his voice husky with emotion.

"I've only been gone for a day," she said.

"Which felt like a thousand years."

Astrid muffled a laugh. Forest and the prince never learned to get along, so she alternated between staying with each of them.

"If I didn't know any better," said the prince. "I'd think that scrawny little man was trying to get you pregnant again."

Astrid rolled her eyes. They had tried several times but none of the attempts were successful, no matter how much she wanted to give Rose a younger sibling.

"Enduring his tiny dick must have made you hot and bothered," rumbled the prince, reaching down to slip a large hand between Astrid's legs. "Let me help you feel better."

Astrid groaned. His touch was electric and the smell of his arousal filled her with desire. She had been waiting for this moment since they said goodbye the day before.

It was difficult for Forest to understand, but she still loved being ravaged by the prince's large body. She loved being held down and fucked senseless in the middle of the woods.

The prince's warm tongue ran up Astrid's bare neck before moving to her mouth. His lips moved across hers without having to think.

Astrid melted into him as her groin flared to life. She groaned and rubbed her thighs together, desperate for more stimulation.

The prince bit down lightly on her lower lip, making her gasp in pleasure. The intensity of the kiss grew even more passionate.

She didn't think that she would ever tire of him.

Astrid pulled away, cheeks burning with anticipation as she slowly started to unbutton her blouse. Her eyes never leaving his, stripping down until she was wearing nothing.

The prince watched her with hungry eyes.

He growled and grabbed her, pushing her up against the cabin as he kissed her neck hungrily. He ground himself against her, making her gasp in pleasure.

Astrid wrapped her legs around him as he entered her.

They moved together in perfect harmony, like animals mating in the wild, raw passion driving them faster and faster towards ecstasy.

Their lovemaking filled the air with an echoing chorus of moans and gasps, his low growls blending with her high-pitched cries of delight.

His deep thrusts sent waves of heat up her body, setting her nerve endings aflame.

They clung to each other until they both reached their climax, then collapsed into a sweaty and exhausted heap on the ground.

As they lay there panting, Astrid couldn't help but smile. She was filled with an intense energy that made everything around them seem brighter and more alive. With contentment filling every inch of her body, she closed her eyes and drifted off to sleep, surrounded by nature's beauty.

It may not have been the life that she dreamed of, but at least they could be together, free to love each other under the starry night sky.

SUBSCRIBE TO BEATRIX STEAM

Subscribe to Beatrix Steam email notifications for future release updates, and get three free ebooks!

www.beatrixsteam.com/subscribe

ALSO BY BEATRIX STEAM

FREE ON KINDLE UNLIMITED

Find more spicy monster romance by Beatrix Steam
at
www.beatrixsteam.com

Bred by my Werewolf Professor

Agatha is hot for her werewolf professor. He constantly rejects her, until his wolf form comes to breed her late one night.

Or does he?

www.beatrixsteam.com/bred

Alien Baby Making Erotica

The king wants his daughter to mate, but she agrees to only sleep with the winner of the alien gladiator tournament. The victor is a large alien warrior who can't wait to thrust his thick pulsing organ inside her, but he'll make sure to pleasure her virgin body first. Plus two more hot erotic alien short stories.

www.beatrixsteam.com/babymaking

Impregnated by the Alien Monster

Lyla will do anything for revenge. That includes being impregnated by a large alien demon in return for power.

Dark sci-fi demon breeding and pregnancy erotica short story for adults 18+. Hardcore alien monster smutt with little plot.

www.beatrixsteam.com/Impregnated

Tentacle Alien Husbands Bundle

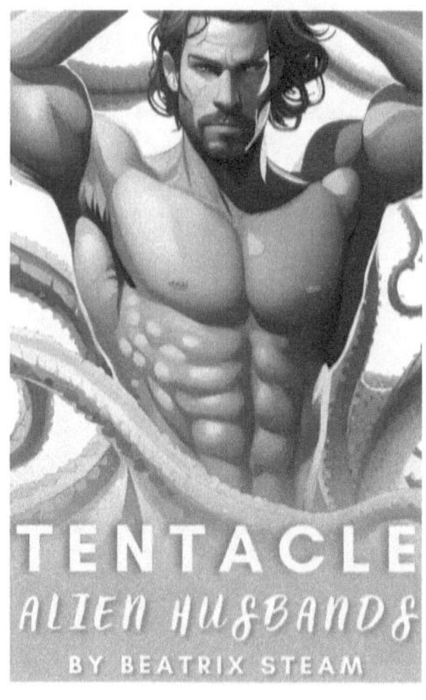

Alien Sam wants nothing more than to marry a hot Korean man, but her tentacle fiancé Hwan isn't willing to let her go.

Plus three more hot tentacle romance short stories to make you wet. Hardcore monster smut with little plot.

www.beatrixsteam.com/husbands

www.ingramcontent.com/pod-product-compliance
Lightning Source LLC
Chambersburg PA
CBHW021357150726
47989CB00005B/2291